Skye Object 3270a

Skye Object 3270a

Linda Nagata

Mythic Island Press LLC
Kula, Hawaii

Skye Object 3270a

Copyright © 2007 by Linda Nagata

This novel was first published by Linda Nagata as a PDF e-book. First mobi electronic edition December 2010.

First print edition February 2011.

ISBN 978-0-9831100-7-1

Mythic Island Press LLC
P.O. Box 1293
Kula, HI 96790-1293

www.mythicislandpress.com

Chapter 1

Skye's skin suit was a royal blue so hot it glowed. It covered every inch of her body, from the toes up, snugging around her like the smooth, thick hide of some water creature. The hood dangled in neat pleats behind her neck. With gloved hands, she reached back and grabbed it, pulling it up and over her short, wispy brown hair, then down across her face. The fabric became clear where it arched over her eyes. Like a living thing squirming into its proper posture, it bent again, to form a stubby muzzle over her nose and mouth. Then it sealed itself at her neckline, the fabric of the hood knitting with the fabric of the suit, so that the seams vanished.

For two seconds there was no fresh air to breath. Then the suit's Dull Intelligence—a machine mind that was fast and functional but not truly self-aware like a human being—spoke to her in its soft, feminine voice, "Activating respiratory function."

Well, it was always nice to breathe. Skye filled her lungs with oxygen-rich air. Then she turned to Zia Adovna, who was standing next to her, wrapped in a glistening gold skin suit. Zia was three days short of her fifteenth birthday and tall for her age. Skye was only five days past her fourteenth, but she was taller. Her grin was invisible inside her hood, but Zia would know. "I'm scared," Skye said. Her suit radio picked up her voice and cast it to Zia on a private link.

Zia's voice murmured into her ears. "And I'm your mother."

They both laughed at the familiar ritual. They'd been sky jumping for almost a year, and it was still a screaming rush every time. A lot simpler than hanging out with guys, and way more exciting.

There were at least two hundred people milling around on the observation platform, though only a few of them had come to jump. Those who were serious were dressed in skin suits. The rest wore street clothes. They lined up at the concession stands, or clustered around the clear bubble that arched over the jump pit, where they could watch set after set of jumpers take off. They blocked Skye's view of the pit, but it didn't matter. She knew that all the jumpers scheduled ahead of them were real people, adults a hundred years old or more. Skye and Zia were adolescents—*ados* in Silken slang, pronounced with twangy long vowels, *a· dæe*, and meaning something like *not old enough to know the difference*.

Skye and Zia were the first ados to jump this morning. All the others had signed up for later slots because they wanted to see if she and Zia really would set a new joint distance record.

Skye smiled to herself. No sweat.

They waited for an elevator to carry them down one level to the pit. When one opened, they stepped aboard. Zia registered them. "Zia Adovna," she announced, and this time her suit radio carried her voice to both Skye and the Dull Intelligence in the jumper's pit. "And Skye Dropped-in-from-Nowhere—"

"Oh, ha ha."

"—on a tandem jump of length 4.3 kilometers. Qualifications on file."

The pit DI responded in a neutral voice: "Zia Adovna and Skye Object 3270a approved for jump, 4.3 kilometers." The doors started to slide closed.

Then the voice of Commandant Penwo, the jump pit supervisor, cut in over their radio link. The doors froze, still half open. "Four point three K?" Penwo said. "Uh-uh, kids. I don't think so."

Zia slapped a symbolic hand over Skye's face mask, before she could respond. Then she answered Penwo in a polite, formal voice. "Is there a problem, Commandant? We have DI approval."

"Sooth, there is a problem. Four point three K is the maximum allowable drop. It's not a kid's jump."

Skye glared at the elevator doors, willing them to close all the way, but they remained half-open. Commandant Penwo was holding them open.

The ados on the observation deck had begun to notice the delay. Heads turned. Questioning looks were aimed in their direction. This was not shaping up into the triumph Skye had imagined. "Commandant," she growled. "We've completed the required preliminaries. We've jumped two point eight klicks. This is the next logical step, and it's only adding six seconds to the drop time."

"Six seconds, one and half kilometers, and a bone-crushing velocity check when you hit the end of your cables. No, Skye. Those regulations were drafted for physically mature ados, not for juveniles—"

"Please check the dates, Commandant," Zia cut in. "Skye Object is officially fourteen."

"And besides, we've earned this," Skye said. "You know we have. We're both fourteen, so it's our decision—"

Skye's argument floundered as a commotion erupted on the observation deck. Her skin suit's external mike picked up the noise. A few ados squealed. More roared with laughter. There was a swirl of motion near the bubble, then a sudden burst of excited chatter. One booming voice rose above it all. "Hey, *Skye*."

Behind her visor, Zia's face scrunched up as if she'd tasted something revolting. Skye groaned, knowing that Buyu-the-brainless had caught up with her once again. "Please, Commandant," she pleaded. "We're legal. Close the doors now, before—"

"Hey Skye," Buyu shouted again, as he shouldered his way out of the crowd. "Did you lose something?"

Buyu was easily the biggest ado boy Skye knew. He was a head taller than her and twice as wide—a walking display of over-developed muscle. On his round face he had recently grown a line of curly hair that exactly traced the outline of his jawbone—a *beard*. Skye hadn't even known what to call it until Zia told her. In Silk, no one wore hair on their faces . . . or no one had, until recently. Now strange little sculpted beards were all the rage among ado boys. Sculpted beards and . . . *nose bells?* Buyu had replaced his nose ring with a little bell that dangled on a clip. Skye could hear its high-pitched tinkling even through the noise of the crowd. She started to giggle . . . until she realized what he held in his hands.

Did you lose something . . . ?

Impaled on his fingers, frantically wriggling to get free, was a mass of gold goo anchoring two whipping tentacles, each half a meter long. Skye's eyes widened in horror as she recognized the mashed body of her robot attendant. "*Ord*," she whispered. It took only a second for her anger to catch up with her surprise. Buyu had gotten his hands on Ord, and he'd smashed it. Even as she watched, the gooey gold plasm of Ord's biogel body dripped and flowed around Buyu's upturned hands. The tentacles whisked over his head like streamers, groping, groping, but never grasping any-thing.

"Open the hood," Skye growled at her suit's Dull Intelligence. Then she stomped out of the elevator.

Zia peeled off her own hood. "Skye!" she shouted. "You can't go now—"

"I'll be right back, okay?"

Then she turned her full anger on Ord's assailant. "Buyu! You vicious brain-dead creep. Put Ord down *now*. What makes you think it's okay to touch my things? Who gave you permission to vandalize my attendant? Did you forget to go for your usual treat-ment at the monkey house?"

Buyu stopped cold, staring at Skye in helpless surprise. The "monkey house" was the name everybody used for the medical center—maybe because the docs believed their most important work had to do with the mind, especially, helping people to hold onto a civil attitude. In a fragile, crowded city nothing was more important than getting along, so the docs sometimes monkeyed around with people's thoughts and attitudes.

Now Buyu's wide brow wrinkled as his gaze shifted to Ord. He looked as if he'd been presented with an unsolvable puzzle. "Skye, I found your robot like this. It dripped out of a ceiling vent, and hit the floor looking like melted glass. It was about to get stomped. So I picked it up."

"Stomped!" Skye did not try to hide her indignation. "Ord never gets stomped. Only grabbed on occasion. And vandalized."

"Skye, it's biogel. Ord's just melted. It's not hurt. Here." He held out his hands, his fingers pointing down, while the blob that was Ord oozed off them. "It'll fix itself as soon as it calms down."

Was he right? Skye leaned forward to catch the flowing plasm in her hands. One tentacle touched her arm and wrapped tight around it.

"You know," Buyu said, "you really should see the monkey house docs about managing your anger."

She glared up at him. "Like you know."

Her gloves reproduced the soft, oozy feel of Ord's shapeless flesh. It steamed a little in the cool air, but Buyu was right. Already she could see the biogel forming into Ord's old shape. She bit her lip, feeling a little embarrassed now. "It was supposed to be locked in Zia's breather."

"Guess it found the ventilation system."

Well, duh. She almost rolled her eyes, but she caught herself. "Well. Thanks for picking it up. I guess." The goo in her palms was quickly reorganizing itself, flowing into the shape of a little square-shouldered bottle with a big, round cap. The cap was Ord's robot head. She watched as two optical disks surfaced, drifting until they took their place as eyes. The tentacles slid into position where arms should be. Two squat legs sprouted in the cooling tissue, and finally, a mouth formed. "Good Skye," Ord said, in its soft, whispery voice. "Come home. Come home now. To jump is bad, Skye. Be safe."

Skye cracked a grin. She couldn't help it. "Don't worry, Ord. You know I always do everything by the rules."

Ord's tentacle tightened around her arm. Out of habit, she started to boost the little robot up to her shoulder, but she froze when she realized Zia was standing beside her. "You know you can't take it with us," Zia warned.

"Sooth," Skye said. "I know."

Ord wasn't made to function in the airless void outside the city. That's why they'd locked it in Zia's breather in the first place.

Skye frowned at the robot clinging to her hand. Ord had been following Skye around the city of Silk since she was seven years old. The robot had been assigned to her by city authority when she'd disappeared once too often from a foster home. It was supposed to be her babysitter, her tutor, her own personal tattle-tale if she ever violated any of Silk's city rules.

She wasn't a juvy anymore, though. Now she was fourteen, a full ado, and if she wanted, she could visit authority offices and ask someone there to decommission Ord. If she wanted.

She sighed, desperately wishing Ord had an off switch, because its first instinct was to be with her, always, no matter what. Sometimes that was endearing, but sometimes it just got in the way.

"Hurry up, Skye," Zia said. "Or we're going to lose our slot."

At this, Ord looked distressed. It shook its little head. "No Skye, no jump," it pleaded. "Please good Skye? Come home?"

"Oh, Ord—"

"Skye!" Zia scolded. "You're not going to let that little worry-wart—"

"Of course not!"

"Then come on."

"But—"

What was she supposed to do with Ord? She didn't want it to follow them onto the elevator. If only Commandant Penwo had closed the doors sooner. Then they would have made it into the jump pit, where Ord could not follow.

Her anxious gaze fell on Buyu. She eyed him suspiciously,

scowling at the line of his beard, and his nose bell. "You said Ord just fell out of the ceiling vent, right?"

Buyu nodded, and his nose bell jingled. "It looked like warm jelly. I guess it had to melt to squeeze out past the baffles."

So he hadn't really hurt it. "Well then, would you mind ... holding on to it one more time?"

Ord was listening. Skye knew that, so before the words were halfway out, she shoved the little robot at Buyu's muscle-bound belly. He raised his hands instinctively, and she jammed Ord into them as quickly as she could. Buyu's fingers closed around the little robot, and immediately it started melting again. Even worse, it still had a tentacle wrapped around Skye's arm. She backed away, prying at the tentacle's adhesive tip. Zia tried to help her. "Would you mind, Buyu?" Skye repeated. "Just until we're on the elevator, okay? You can let it go after that."

Buyu juggled the warm mass in his hands, a goofy grin on his face. "Sure, Skye. I'll do what I can, but hey, you've got to get it all the way off you first."

"We're trying!" Zia snapped.

The tentacle had stretched so far now, Skye feared it might break. She stamped a booted foot. "Ord, you listen to me! Let go right *now*." She jerked her hand back hard, and to her surprise, the tentacle popped free. Skye staggered backward. Zia whooped. Had Ord really obeyed her? No. It was more likely the robot had just reached the point where it couldn't stretch any more.

"Skye, come *on*," Zia growled, pulling her toward the waiting elevator.

Skye stumbled after her, still off-balance. She glanced back, to see Ord flowing out of Buyu's hands in a long, golden honey drip that puddled on the floor. "Hey, Buyu, *thanks!*" Then she turned and sprinted after Zia.

But in that glance back, she'd seen Buyu's brown cheeks flush in a rosy, embarrassed warmth. Buyu, embarrassed? That was a first. Skye didn't want to think about the reason. She didn't want to think about that at all.

She didn't stop running until she hit the back of the elevator with a concussion that rattled her teeth. Then she grabbed her hood and pulled it back over her head. This time, Penwo closed the doors.

Skye sighed as the familiar hum of air being pumped out of the elevator car reached her through the skin suit. As the air pressure inside the car dropped close to zero she felt her suit stiffen, but the sensation passed in a couple of seconds. Her skin suit was made of tens of thousands of tiny scales, each continuously talking with all the rest as they slid against one another *allowing* Skye's body to move. That was the key to the suit's operation: it detected Skye's motions and flexed to match them, rather like a wall, constantly folding to get out of her way. It had to be that strong, to keep her safe in the airless vacuum outside the city.

In a high, teasing voice, Zia said, "Would you mind, Buyu? *Please* Buyu."

Skye groaned, and leaned against the wall of the elevator. "Did I really sound like that?" she whispered over their private link.

"Well, ado, let's just say you were under stress."

Skye thought she might die of embarrassment—but at least the elevator was moving. It dropped only a single floor. Then the doors opened onto the jump pit.

The pit was an ugly chunk of a room, weirdly lit by panels set between the three sets of elevator doors along its curving back wall. Faint shadows shifted and rippled across the floor, leading Skye to glance up, at the domed observation bubble, and the faces of nearly two hundred ados staring down at her. Buyu was there, though he no longer had Ord. He gave her a thumbs-up. Skye pretended not to see.

She straightened her shoulders, glancing nervously at Commandant Penwo's office, sheltered behind a transparent wall on one side of the jump pit. She could see him, dressed in street clothes and rocking in a high-back chair. He didn't look happy. He wanted to veto this jump, but Skye was fourteen now, and by Silk's city charter that meant she was free to do any activity approved for ados. It was a giddy freedom that she had been cherishing over the five days since her birthday.

Penwo caught her glance. He shook his head. "Somewhere between six and sixty people lose their good sense," he said. "We don't call this phase 'dumb ado' for nothing."

Skye's fingers twitched. "Can you remember that far back, Commandant?"

Penwo grinned. "Have fun, Skye Object. Hope you live."

"Forever."

Usually, it was necessary to wait on the floor of the jump pit while other jumpers took their turn. This time, though, they'd been delayed so long the floor was clear. Skye was glad of it. She didn't like waiting under any circumstances, but especially not when she'd been toasted by embarrassment. Her body was screaming for a jump. There was no better way to scare out all the cramped, ugly feelings everybody stored up from day to day.

With Zia, she loped across the jump pit, stopping at the railing that guarded the abyss. Skye's gloved hands closed on the top rail. Her booted toes curled over the edge, yet she had no sensation of any great height. She wouldn't get that until she looked down. For now, she looked across the abyss, twenty meters to a massive, curving wall.

It was the wall of the elevator column.

In Silk, when people talked about the elevator column, they were never referring to the puny machines that ran between the city's industrial levels, or that carried people up and down inside the high rises that studded the city's outer slope. This elevator column was far larger than any of those. It was a space elevator, a massive cable that rose from the surface of the planet called Deception Well, all the way up through the atmosphere and into the airless vacuum of space beyond. Tens of thousands of kilometers separated its beginning from its end. The elevator cars that moved up and down this long highway were the size of multistory buildings, and a journey to the top took days.

The space elevator was a beautiful balancing act. It could stand only because the downward pull of Deception Well's gravity exactly equaled the outward pull on the mammoth counterweight at the column's end.

On the whole column only one point was actually in orbit. That was at PSO—planetary synchronous orbit, a point high on the column where a freely-orbiting satellite would require exactly one day to complete one trip around the planet. Above PSO, any object dropped from the elevator would fall away from the planet. Below that point, a dropped object would plunge downward into Deception Well.

Skye smiled. That was why it was possible to jump. The city of Silk was built on the elevator column. Like a bead on a string, it dangled 300 kilometers above the surface of Deception Well.

She leaned against the rail. There was no danger. The railing would curl to catch her if she started to go over before she was tethered. Or so the real people promised. Skye wanted to test the system, but she knew she'd lose jumping privileges for half a year if she ever tried it, so she curbed her curiosity.

Two blisters inflated in the surface of the elevator column. Skye braced herself, as a cable shot out of each of them, moving with the speed of a chameleon's tongue. One hit her in the belly with a feather-touch of pressure. A thin gold cord spooled off the cable's end, sliding into a socket on her royal blue suit. "Compatibility check in progress," the suit DI announced. "Ten, nine, eight . . ."

As the countdown proceeded, the other cable reached Zia, and linked to her skin suit.

The cables were a color between gold and copper, shimmering in the weird, angled light of the jump pit. This close, it was easy to see that they were made of thin, tightly coiled cord. They flexed and stretched like living things.

As the countdown finished, Skye found herself bouncing up and down on the balls of her feet. "Compatibility check complete," the DI announced. "Integration at one hundred percent."

"You're too close together," Commandant Penwo complained. "Space yourselves, until you're at least twenty meters apart, or I can't give you clearance."

"Fus-sy," Zia muttered, but they each took a few steps to the side.

"That's it then," Penwo said. "Do be sure to jump straight, ladies, because you are going to have a long, long fall, and that means a long, long time to tangle your lines."

"We know the dynamics," Skye muttered.

"I hope so. Cleared to jump."

Zia whooped. Skye grinned, glancing overhead one more time at the ados watching through the observation bubble. A few of them were jumping up and down. More were pumping their fists, their mouths moving as if they were chanting something. Zia raised a hand in greeting, like a soccer star walking onto the field, but Skye felt horribly self-conscious. All she could bring herself to do was look down.

The elevator column looked like a huge, slightly curving wall. Below the jump pit it was bathed in sunlight. Skye's gaze followed it down, down, down. Massive at first, it tapered slowly with distance, until she couldn't see it anymore, as it plunged into the glowing green crescent of Deception Well's equatorial continent, over 300 kilometers below.

Three hundred kilometers straight down.

If the cable failed, Skye knew she would not stop falling until she burned up in the atmosphere.

Her heart ran fast. Her skin felt hot with a sweat that was wicked away by her skin suit almost before it could form. Skye drew a deep breath, then she turned to catch Zia's eye. "Ready ado?"

"Ready," Zia echoed. "On three. One. Two. Three."

Still holding each other's gaze, they dove together, head-first off the platform.

Chapter 2

*A*cceleration.

Skye felt as if an invisible hand had reached up from the planet and grabbed her, pulling her down, faster, and faster, in a sublime dive. Black lines had been painted on the massive wall of the elevator column, so it was easy to see her speed increase, until the lines all blurred together and all she was aware of was an overwhelming rush.

There was nothing here to slow her down.

Close to the planet, air would have slowed her plunge. She would have reached terminal velocity—the maximum speed that she could reach—in only a few seconds and the thrill would be over. But above the atmosphere there was nothing to hold her back . . . except the thin gold cord feeding out behind her.

The wall of the elevator column flashed in a stroboscopic mix of silver and black. The glare of daylight from the planet was blinding. She could see Zia, twenty meters away, soaring head-down, her arms tight against her sides. She could hear Zia over her suit radio, flying downward on a jubilant howl.

They had never jumped so far before, or fallen with such speed. The equations played like music in Skye's head. In five seconds they would fall a tenth of a kilometer, but double the time to ten seconds, and the distance would quadruple to four tenths of a kilometer as Deception Well's gravity pulled them down ever faster.

Fifteen seconds → *one kilometer*
Twenty seconds → *1.8 kilometers*
Twenty-five seconds → *2.8 kilometers*
Thirty seconds → *4.0 kilometers*
Thirty-one seconds → *4.3 kilometers*

No one jumped farther than four point three kilometers. Not the most experienced sky jumper in the city, because that was the limit of tolerance of the jump cable.

Thirty one seconds passed much too soon—and hit hard.

Skye was falling at over 250 meters per second—or over 900 kilometers an hour—when the cord reached its limit. It yanked tight. Zia's cry of glory snapped off like a broken stick while Skye felt crushed, a fly slammed flat under a swatting hand. She couldn't breathe. Her bones might have been pulverized, her brain flattened. And still she was falling. The stripes on the column continued to flash past, though ever more slowly now as the cord stretched and stretched, uncoiling to absorb her momentum, until at last, she stopped.

She did not bounce back up, but the thrill ride wasn't over yet. Her plunge had carried her away from the column. Now, hanging from the end of the taut cord, she swung back in toward the silver wall. It rushed up at her. She scrambled to grab the cord, pulling herself upright so that she slammed into the wall feet first. Her skin suit hardened to receive the blow and still she felt as if she'd been dropped from Old Guard Heights. Her ears buzzed, and darkness loomed in her vision. She thought she was going to pass out.

Maybe she did.

When next she looked, she discovered that her gloves and the hot zones on her shins had knitted to the wall, gluing her in place. She couldn't remember that happening. "Zia . . . ?"

Panic seized her, as she realized Zia was not at her side. She leaned away from the wall, her gaze searching the vast, bright expanse. *There.* Skye spotted Zia's golden skin suit, far away around the curve of the elevator column. She looked like a speck. Some gaudy fly resting a moment before it flew again . . .

"Zia!"

"Skye . . . ?" Zia sounded as rattled as Skye felt. "You . . . okay?"

"Sooth. Or anyway, I'll fix."

"Hey ado," Zia said softly. "We did it."

"Yeah." Skye's body ached with victory. So why did she feel disappointed?

She leaned back, looking up the elevator column to try to spot the crawl cart that would pick them up. From this perspective, the base of the city looked like a distant parasol gleaming in the sunlight, surrounded by the black void of space. Not so much different, really, than it looked from two point eight kilometers. Except smaller.

A flash of motion drew her eye. The crawl cart. It was skimming down its narrow track, still maybe a kilometer away. Skye squinted, and thought she could make out another jumper inside it. She spoke to her suit DI, "Hark. Release right hand." The hot zone on her glove switched off, and her hand came unstuck from the wall. She reached up to wave hello—and the sky exploded. A fierce white flash punched through the darkness beyond the city, like a tiny sun, flaring into dazzling life, than fading almost instantly.

"Yeah!" Zia whooped. "Did you see that?"

Skye was suddenly aware of the hard pounding of her heart. "What was it?"

"Something big! The meteor defense lasers hit it. We were lucky to see it. I've never even heard of anything that big falling out of the nebula."

Skye squinted, trying to see past the city's glare. At night the sky above Silk would glow with the thin, milky light of Kheth's nebula, a veil of dust and tiny stones that surrounded the inner system. The debris was all that was left of Kheth's other planets, destroyed in some ancient alien war, long, long before humans had even evolved from their primate ancestors on distant Earth. Tiny life forms lived among the debris. They were called butterfly gnomes because of their wing-like solar panels. Sometimes the nebula's particles would brush against one another and stick, to form a larger stone. But before the clusters could grow to more than a few grams, the butterfly gnomes would discover them, and use an electric charge to blast them apart again. Now and then though, the gnomes failed, and an occasional pebble would escape the nebula and wander into the inner-system. The city's meteor defense lasers were always on guard against bits of debris that might strike the city. Skye had seen them flash hundreds of times before, but never with such brilliance. "Zia, there's no way the butterfly gnomes would have missed an object that big."

"Hmm. Maybe it was an asteroid that's been wandering around the inner system for the last few eons. Or maybe it was a chunk from the swan burster."

The swan burster was a great ring, 3000 kilometers across, that orbited Deception Well like a dark moon. The dead remnant of an alien weapon, it was estimated to be thirty million years old. Only twenty years ago its surface had been shattered in a collision. Fragments of the swan burster had been spinning through the inner system ever since.

"Is there anything else it could have been?" Zia asked. "There's not much out there . . ."

"There is one other thing," Skye said softly.

Zia's voice grew sharp with suspicion. "What are you thinking, ado?"

"Well . . ." Skye hesitated, afraid to say it, afraid that by saying it she might somehow make it true. "We know the butterfly gnomes don't attack animate matter. . . ."

Living things were animate, their tissues busily interacting at the scale of atoms and molecules. A lot of manufactured objects were animate too, made of smart molecules that responded to the environment around them. Ord was animate matter. So was a skin suit. So were the hulls of most spacecraft.

Skye swallowed against a throat made dry by fear. "Zia, maybe it was another lifeboat . . . like the one that brought *me* here."

—∿∿∿—

Skye had dropped out of nowhere.

No one knew where she had come from. Thirteen years ago an astronomer had seen a gleam on the outer edge of the nebula. Days passed, and the light grew brighter. A solar sail, already a full kilometer across, was growing from the animate hull of a tiny incoming spacecraft.

The solar sail was huge, but it was thinner than aluminum foil. It was designed to catch sunlight the way a boat's sail would catch the wind, using the pressure of light to slow the tiny lifeboat that it carried. But as the sail swept through the nebula it was bombarded by pebbles and flecks of dust that tore its fragile sheet faster than the sail could heal and re-grow. By the time a research ship reached the lifeboat a year had elapsed and only a few shreds remained of the once-bright fabric.

Within the lifeboat, the researchers discovered the frozen body of a nameless two year old girl. All the records aboard her vessel had been erased. There was no way to know how long she had been in cold sleep, if it had been two years or two hundred . . . or more. There was no way to know who had put her in the lifeboat, or why. When the researchers revived her, she had only a two-year-old's fuzzy memory.

They had named her after the astronomer's designation for her lifeboat, Sky Object 3270a, adding only an *e* to her first name.

—∿∿∿—

"It wasn't another lifeboat," Zia said. "If the object was that big, someone would have spotted it."

"Maybe."

Skye was not at all convinced. Lifeboats were dark. In the light-less deeps of space they were almost impossible to see. They were made that way, because the only reason to use one was for escape.

For centuries, people had moved outward from Earth, making

homes on new worlds that circled alien suns. Now and again, they found fossil traces of long vanished civilizations, but nothing else, until the frontier had been pushed a thousand years from home . . . and then they found the Chenzeme warships.

It was a terrible discovery. The robotic Chenzeme vessels might have been thousands, even millions of years old. There were no aliens aboard them. Machine minds steered the ships, and ordered them to attack any vessel that was not of their own kind.

No one knew for sure why Skye was in the lifeboat, but everyone could guess. She had probably been born on a great ship, like a self-contained city tower faring across the sky, carrying human passengers on a hundred year voyage from one star to another. A great ship was an irresistible target for a prowling Chenzeme warship. When it seemed certain they would come under the warship's guns, Skye's parents must have put her aboard a lifeboat.

As the lifeboats were ejected, most of them would have been spotted and destroyed by the Chenzeme pursuer—but at least one had escaped, to drift (*for how many centuries?*) until it encountered the nebula that sheltered Deception Well, and its star, called Kheth.

I can't be the only survivor.

City Authority didn't agree. "It's a miracle even you made it here," they told her, over and over again.

She stared into the darkness beyond the city. The glare of sunlight on the elevator column was so bright she could not see any stars, only the silvery tower of the column rising, rising as if to infinity, dwindling finally to a thread as it disappeared from sight.

The Silkens had never looked very hard for other lifeboats. Maybe they just didn't want to find them.

Chapter 3

Stop sulking," Zia said, as they sipped an icy slush at a balcony table. It was near-noon, and the grand walk was crowded with lunch time throngs.

Skye leaned back in her chair, turning her face to a cool breeze that swept up the city's slope. Like Zia, she had changed from her skin suit into shorts and a light shirt. "I'm not sulking."

Zia scowled. "So what do you call this? Celebrating? You haven't stopped brooding since the crawl cart picked us up."

Skye had stood at the crawl cart's railing, her gaze fixed on the brilliant white clouds so far below, and the crystal blue of the ocean. She had hardly heard the congratulations of the other jumpers who climbed aboard the cart as it worked its way back up to the city. She'd been happy to see Ord, though. The little robot had met them at the gate, looking no worse for its encounter with Buyu. Its tentacles had wrapped happily around Skye's wrist. Now it lurked under the table. Skye felt Ord's gentle, reassuring taps against her ankle, but she was not comforted.

"I'm not brooding," she said after a minute. "I'm just . . . thinking."

"So stop it. It's not good for you."

Skye smiled. "Careful," she said, "or I'm going to start confusing you with Buyu."

Zia took a mock swipe at her head. Skye ducked, and one of the drinks almost went over. A woman at the next table gave them a sour look. Zia shrugged and picked up her slush. Then she leaned back, resting her knees against the railing. "Let's go over this one more time. That which went *flash* was a fragment of the swan burster, just like I said. City Authority had been tracking it for years. There was an announcement in the media this morning, predicting today's lightshow, and if we hadn't been so caught up in our jump, we might have heard about it. So that which went *flash* was not a lifeboat, so cheer up."

"There could be lifeboats out there," Skye said.

Zia started breathing heavily, her teeth gritted in cartoon rage, but she stopped fast when a couple of ado boys came by their table to offer congratulations. Zia chatted them up, while Skye leaned on the balcony rail, gazing down at the long slope of the cone-shaped city.

Silk hung on the elevator cable like a bead on a string—or maybe like a cone-shaped mountain with the thread of the elevator cable running through its core. At 300 kilometers above Deception Well, it was far beyond the atmosphere, yet all the houses, apartment buildings, parks, and walkways were on the outside slopes. People could live in the light because they were protected from the airless vacuum of space by a transparent, self-repairing canopy that rose over the city like a bubble, held up by the pressure of air.

The grand walk encircled the city's highest, narrowest level. From the restaurant balcony, Skye could look down past the low-rise buildings of Ado Town to the green belt of Splendid Peace Park, 600 meters below. She waited until the boys moved off. Then she said, "You think I'm crazy, because I believe there could be other lifeboats out there."

"I don't think you're crazy. I think you just don't want to be, well . . . alone. You know you're not alone."

"Sooth. Zia, the point is we don't know if there are any more . . . like me. Because no one's looked."

Zia crossed her arms over her chest. "So why don't you look?"

"Huh?"

"Instead of whining about it, why don't *you* go look?"

"How?"

"How should I know? I just know that if it's more important to you than to anyone else, you should be doing it."

Skye was already nodding, as ideas sprouted in her head. "Ord!"

"Yes, Skye?" The little robot poked its head over the far rim of the table. "Order food now?"

"No. Forget lunch. Remember the article you found for us on the swan burster fragment?"

"Lunch forgotten, Skye. Article remembered."

Zia choked on her drink as Ord started to recite the article in full. Skye smiled. "Good Ord. Don't read it to me again, okay? Just tell me who wrote it."

"Author credit, Devi Hand, Astronomical Society."

Skye winked at Zia. Then, using the formal address for real people—*Maturus*—meaning "fully aged" and abbreviated simply as "M," she said, "M. Hand tracked that swan burster fragment. Maybe M. Hand might also have something to say about tracking lifeboats."

"Do you think he'd be interested in talking to ados? He's probably five hundred years old."

Skye shrugged. "I don't know, but it won't hurt to ask. Let's go find him."

"When?"

"Now."

"Uh-uh." Zia shook her head. "Work."

"Oh. Sooth." Skye frowned.

The people of Silk counted days in groups of six, for no better reason than that it suited them. So Skye and Zia had classes for three mornings, and then they were off for three mornings. Most of the afternoons they worked as interns—student helpers rotating through different professions, exploring their world from the inside out.

Zia was presently working with a team of planetary biologists. Skye was studying nanotechnology. Usually she enjoyed every minute spent under the tutelage of Yan, learning a branch of engineering in which matter was shaped atom by atom, to build precise structures that ranged from simple threads of pure diamond fiber to tiny, complex, programmable nanomachines called Makers that patrolled the human body, defending it against disease and the breakdown that had once been caused by aging. Once, people had died after only seventy or eighty years of life. Skye had a hard time imagining such a thing, but Yan insisted it was so. "Without Makers to keep us healthy, our bodies would quickly wear down and eventually fail. It's our Makers that allow us to go on living past our first hundred years." Past adolescence, that is. In Silk, no one was considered fully adult—or truly *real*—until they were at least a century old.

Yan himself was 274-years-old. He'd been one of the original immigrants to Silk, arriving at the age of two, a baby in cold sleep, just like Skye. Except he'd come on a great ship, accompanied by his parents, and they had all been revived together.

Despite his years, Yan looked as youthful and healthy as any adult. The age of real people showed only in their eyes, that seemed to see deeper than ado eyes, and in their outlook. Skye had a hard time describing exactly what that outlook was, but it had much to do with the confidence, the patience, the self-assurance they all seemed to possess. They had seen and done so much that they often seemed to know exactly what would happen next. It was a trait she found by turns annoying or reassuring, depending on her mood.

Yan was generous enough not to teach her too much, allowing her to form her own opinions as she explored nature at the molecular scale. She loved seeing the structure of the world made real around her, feeling the strength of bonds between atoms that joined to form molecules. It made her feel as if the mystery of existence was unfolding at her command.

She drew in a deep breath, then let it go in a long sigh. "I want to do everything at once! Why does it always feel like there's never enough time?"

"Easy, ado," Zia said. "We'll fit it all in. We work now. Meanwhile, we let Ord hunt down M. Hand and make an appointment for us. Real people like to be formal, after all." She reached under the table and caught Ord by one of its stubby legs, hauling the little robot out, while the leg stretched to twice its normal length. "Can you handle it, pet?" she asked, dropping Ord on the table. "Find this M. Devi Hand for us, and see if he's willing to meet"— She turned back to Skye, with a questioning look—"when?"

"Tonight," Skye said, as Ord rearranged its golden tissue, and stood on the table top, reclaiming an attitude of dignity. "Ord, see if you can get us an appointment for tonight, okay?"

"Yes Skye. Not too late though."

Zia rolled her eyes. "And Ord, *try* not to embarrass us by sounding like such an annoying little babysitter, okay?"

Chapter 4

Ord had gotten the appointment with M. Hand, report-ing the astronomer to be delighted at their interest in his work. "Rare enough for ados," was the phrase the little robot reproduced for them in a soft, masculine voice. Skye wrinkled her nose, wondering if she should feel flattered or insulted at this comment. Then she decided it didn't matter. M. Hand would see them, and this evening too. He had invited both of them to his home.

So after work Skye waited for Zia as they'd agreed, by the koi pond in Splendid Peace Park. The park encircled the base of the city like a green skirt, and all the neighborhoods spilled down the city slopes to touch on it somewhere in its circuit. She watched as three musicians set up their instruments near the water. The day was drawing to a close. Kheth's light spilled at a sharp angle over the city's rim, so that the musicians' shadows ran all the way across the pond, and beyond.

Zia was late.

Several picnickers arrived, laying out blankets on the grass. Skye felt hungry watching them. She stood on her toes, to see if she could spot Zia coming down the trail from the city library, but all she saw was a little boy out walking his dokey. The furry creature looked a little like a dog. It strolled beside the boy, hardly as high as his calf.

Like the dogs Skye had seen in the VR, the dokey walked on four legs, but it also had two more limbs in front, both with little monkey-like hands. Its face was round and alert, like a flying fox. Most of its body was covered with short, thick, brown fur, except behind its ears where there sprouted tufts of green fur, and on its tail, where long green hair shimmered with every wag.

The first dokey had been created only three years ago, as a class project in a genetic engineering course. Now they were everywhere, the only kind of pet city authority had ever allowed people to have. Skye knelt, careful to keep her skirt out of the grass. She didn't usually wear dresses, but she had decided on one tonight because most real people appreciated a formal style. She patted her knee and smiled at the dokey. The little creature came bounding over to her. Its hands kneaded the shimmery hem of her skirt, while she stroked the soft tufts of green fur behind its ears. "It sure is cute," she told the boy.

Ord picked that moment to slip out from behind a low gardenia hedge. "Message, Skye," it announced.

"From who?" The dokey had turned belly-up, encouraging her to stroke the soft brown fur on its underside.

"Zia Adovna," Ord said. "Play it now?"

Skye groaned, knowing it had to be bad news. She chucked the dokey under the chin, then stood up. The boy clucked at his little pet. It scrambled to its feet, then leaped for his hand, climbing from there onto his shoulder. "Thanks," Skye told him. The boy waved and walked on while she turned to Ord with a sigh of resignation. "Okay. Play it."

So Ord started talking, mimicking Zia's voice exactly: "Bad news, ado. I'm due at my dad's tonight. I forgot it was his birthday.

You're invited of course! Have Ord reschedule our appointment with M. Hand for tomorrow, okay?"

Skye's hands knotted into fists. "*Zeme dust!*" she cursed. "Of all the nights!"

Why did things have to fall out like this? She liked Zia's dad. He was a lydra farmer who cloned the tentacled beasts used in zero-gravity construction. On any other night she would have been happy to stop by and help celebrate.

But it wasn't any other night.

Skye looked at Ord. "Let's get something to eat," she said. "And then you and I, we can go see M. Hand ourselves. How does that sound?"

"Sounds sweet," Ord crooned. "Sounds nice. Home early. Good Skye."

Full dark had fallen by the time Skye followed Ord past the exclusive district of Old Guard Heights to the equally exclusive complex of three tapering white towers called the Ice Sisters. Ord made to enter the lobby of the tallest Sister, but Skye hesitated. "Ord, are you sure this is the right address?" Only the oldest of the real people lived in these towers. It was said some of them never came out.

"Yes Skye. Please come."

The lobby was empty. Ord called the elevator. It was glass, and as it rose up the tower's outer face Skye felt as if the city was falling away from her feet. *Like jumping in reverse.* It carried her all the way to the top without stopping.

When the doors opened, she stepped out into a dimly lit alcove. It opened onto a wide balcony populated with tall, tropical shrubs and small flowering trees, all growing in neat planters. Through the foliage she glimpsed the formal double doors of an exclusive apartment. No hint of light leaked through the glass panes, and she began to wonder if M. Hand had forgotten her appointment. Perhaps no one was home?

The Dull Intelligence that served as major-domo for the apartment quickly banished that doubt. "Welcome, Mistress Object!" it called in a cheery masculine voice that emanated from somewhere above the elevator doors. "Your host awaits you on the roof. He asks that you please follow the footlights to the stairway."

Dim lights on the floor came to life, illuminating a slate path that wound through the shrubbery before curving out of sight. Skye nodded nervously—"All right"—but she kept a close watch on Ord, looking for any sign of tension or alarm. She trusted the little robot to know if something was suspect, or wrong, but Ord showed no concern as it scuttled beside her.

An ornate metal railing encircled the balcony. Skye was tempted to look over, for she could hear music and voices drifting up from far below, but the path guided her away to the other side of the rooftop. From here she could look up to the city's summit, and beyond it to the elevator column, its far end still glistening in Kheth's light. Only a few stars were visible within the faint, milky wash of the nebula. The distant, ruined swan burster was a black circle drawn against that luminous sky.

She found the stairs behind a stand of dwarf banana trees. They rose in a single, narrow flight to a flat roof. She craned her neck, straining to see what might be up there, but all she could make out was a railing like the one that ringed the balcony. On the stairs, the footlights were dull red, dimming steadily with each step.

Well.

Skye drew in a deep breath of the flower-scented air. Then she straightened her shoulders and cautiously mounted the stairs. Halfway up, she paused again. Now she could just see the rooftop. It was fully encircled by the railing. No plants grew there. Skye saw only a single shadowy figure, hunched in a chair, peering intently into the eyepiece of a telescope longer than her arm.

"Hello," Skye said softly. "M. Hand?"

"Come quickly! You've almost missed it."

The figure at the telescope neither looked at her, nor sat up. His left hand though, circled in a gesture that clearly said *Come here*. Skye looked around for Ord, but the little robot had disappeared into the shadows. So she swallowed her misgivings and went to join the astronomer, telling herself that real people were supposed to be eccentric, and that M. Hand could be expected to be especially odd, as he must be among the oldest of the old to own such a fine apartment.

As she drew near, the astronomer slid gracefully out of his chair. Skye tried to get a look at his face, but it was very dark here, high above the city. When he bent to check the telescope's mount, long, light-colored hair slipped in loops across his cheek. "Quickly," he said. "Sit down and look. It'll pass out of sight soon."

Skye sat. She leaned forward, careful not to touch the telescope. It perched on the railing with bird-feet, its barrel pointed close to the horizon. She squirmed a little to get just the right position. Then she looked through the eye piece.

She gasped.

The field of view was bisected by a line of bright, sparkling objects. She counted six, eight, twelve spots of jewel-like light. "What is this? I never saw a line of stars like that. They look so close and bright."

"Stars?" He sounded puzzled. "That's the construction zoo."

She sat up abruptly, squinting along the top of the telescope, trying to see the speckles with her own eyes. *There.* A thumb's length above the horizon. She could just make them out if she didn't look directly at them. They appeared to be below the city, dropping toward the dark rim of Deception Well.

The construction zoo was a site in an extremely high orbit, farther out than the end of the elevator cable, where a great ship was being slowly fabricated. The ship-building had begun only five years ago, and it would be many years more before it was completed. For now the great ship existed as separate pieces growing slowly larger as raw materials were carried up the elevator column.

Also to be found in the construction zoo was a habitat for the small work crew, along with several gigantic tentacled lydra, the "construction beasts" that did most of the assembly. Somewhere among all those other things was the lifeboat in which Skye first arrived, for city authority had decided it should be stored in the zoo.

She looked through the telescope again, studying the beautiful line of objects for a few seconds more. Then she turned to M. Hand, not trying to disguise her disappointment. "It all looks so small. I thought you'd be able to see so much more. How did you ever track that fragment of the swan burster?"

"Oh. Well, not with this instrument. This is just a little hobby telescope I . . . I built it when I was twelve. The city's two primary telescopes are both in orbit."

So this was an antique instrument. She wondered how many centuries old it might be. "So you tracked the fragment with the . . . *primary* telescopes?"

"Well, no." His voice was soft and low and almost . . . uncertain? She still could not make out the features of his face. "Actually, the fragments were all located and tagged in the first few years after the swan burster was hit, so all I did was track the signals from this particular fragment. The challenge came in predicting when its orbital path would bring it close to the city—close enough to stimulate the defensive lasers, you see?"

She did, only too well. "So you didn't actually find the fragment at all?"

"No. That was all done before . . . well, it was done before I was born. I wish I'd been in on it."

"Before you were born? But the swan burster was shattered only twenty years ago." As soon as she said it, she understood. Her hand went to her mouth in a futile attempt to stifle a giggle.

"What?" M. Hand demanded.

"Nothing," she choked out. "Sorry. Except . . . I thought you were some awesome old man." And she started giggling all over again.

"Oh. It doesn't matter. Does it?"

Skye's humor vanished as she remembered why she had come. "Actually, I think it does, M.—" She caught herself. She was not going to address him formally if he was only a dumb ado like her. "What was your first name?"

"Devi." He said it quickly, as if afraid it might turn on him, or get away.

"Devi," she repeated. "I think it does matter. I wanted to talk to the person who found the fragments. The person who picked them out of the dark."

"Oh. That would be Tannasen. He helped me with my project, but he's not in the city now. He spends most of his time aboard *Spindrift*."

"The research ship." Skye shivered as vague memories surfaced. Her lifeboat had been found by *Spindrift*. She'd spent over a year aboard the tiny ship, though for most of that time she'd been kept in cold sleep. Tannasen had brought her to consciousness only in the last two weeks before *Spindrift* returned to Silk. She'd been hardly two years old, so almost the only thing she could remember was being afraid.

Devi stirred. "What did you want of Tannasen? If you don't mind my asking?"

Skye wrinkled her nose. Devi was an ado. At most he was only a few years older than her, yet he spoke like the formal old man she had expected to find. "I wanted to ask him how small objects are found. Can a telescope like this—"

"Oh no. It'd be hard even for the big orbital scopes to see a piece of the swan burster after all these years. The fragments don't reflect light." He leaned over the telescope, gazing along its line. "Look at the construction zoo again before it sets. All those objects are gleaming bright because they're lit up by Kheth. The city is in the planet's shadow, so it's night for us. But the construction zoo's orbit is so high it's still in the light. Everything that reflects that light is highly visible. The only object that doesn't reflect light is the lifeboat that was picked up several years ago. If you watch the construction zoo long enough, you can sometimes see one of the lights dim, or even go out. That happens when the lifeboat drifts across your line of sight, blocking the view of the brighter object, *eclipsing* it. If that didn't happen from time to time, it would be impossible to tell the lifeboat was there . . . at least with a scope like this."

"That's right," Skye whispered. "Lifeboats don't reflect light." Of course they could not be seen with a telescope. Why hadn't she thought of that before?

"Are you all right?" Devi asked.

She shook her head, glad that it was dark. "Were you . . . going to say more about the lifeboat?"

"Oh. Right. Well, lifeboats were made to be hard to see. They were for escape, after all."

Sooth.

The great ship must have been under attack. Lifeboats were filled and launched, in the hope that a few might escape the guns of the Chenzeme ship.

Or so she imagined. She had no memory of those days. If she thought hard on it, she could remember the feel of her mother's hands, or the sound of her father's voice, but she could not remember an attack, she could not remember being put aboard the lifeboat, and she could not remember saying goodbye.

"How did Tannasen find the swan burster fragments?" she asked. "If they could not be seen?"

"He used radar. He built a small dish antenna, and launched it into the swan burster's orbit. The antenna sends out pulses of radio waves. Then it listens, to see if any echoes come back. If there's an echo, then there must be an object out there, reflecting the radio waves. One pass won't yield much information, but the antenna can sweep the area over and over again, until a detailed image is assembled. Like waving a flashlight in a dark room."

Skye imagined probing beams of radio waves searching the dust and pebbles of the nebula, feeling for the presence of a lifeboat. It could work. "How can I get permission to use radar?"

Devi laughed. "Study astronomy for a century or two, I guess. There's a huge waiting list for all the equipment. Why do you ask? The fragments from the swan burster have all been tagged. What else is there to find?"

Skye felt a sudden heat in her cheeks. "Maybe nothing, but . . . there might be other lifeboats, like the one I came in."

"You . . . ?" Devi's voice skidded to a high note. "Then you're . . . ?"

"Skye Object 3270a. Yes."

"I thought your name was Zia."

"Zia's my friend. She was supposed to come with me tonight. She couldn't make it, and ... I'm the one who really wants to know, anyway."

He was silent for several seconds. Then, "Let's go somewhere else, okay? And we can talk."

Chapter 5

They walked around to the dark glass doors of the apartment. "Just a minute," Devi said.

He touched the door handle and the apartment's interior flooded with light. Through the glass panes Skye saw an exquisitely decorated living room, with red and gold carpets and black furnishings. Then her gaze shifted. For the first time, Devi was in the light. He was wearing gray slacks, with a black sweater and boots. His hair was bi-colored—an even mix of dark brown and red strands, tied in a loose ponytail behind his neck. He had given in to the ado boy fad for beards: there was a small triangle of dense, rusty-red fuzz on his chin. Heavy brown eyebrows sheltered almond-shaped eyes. The irises were green, flecked with gold. He smiled at Skye. "I'll be right back." Then he stepped inside.

A streak of purple shot out from under a table, hitting Devi in the back of the knee. He stumbled. Skye heard him shout. Then the streak slowed down, resolving into a purple and gold dokey that leaped to Devi's outstretched hand. He turned around to Skye and held his hand out for her to see. The little six-limbed creature clambered and swayed as it pulled itself upright. Devi shrugged helplessly. "Do you mind?"

Skye laughed. "Not at all. What's its name?"

"Jem. He's from the second batch of dokeys ever made. I've had him since . . . since I was thirteen." Jem had climbed up around Devi's shoulders. The dokey started patting his long, straight hair, pinching together the red strands.

Dokeys had been created only three years ago. Skye put the facts together. "So you're sixteen?" she said as he returned to the balcony.

"Yes. Major domo? Call the elevator."

"Yes, master Devi. The elevator will arrive in twenty two seconds."

"Did you really build that telescope yourself?" Skye asked.

He shrugged, while she reached up to scratch Jem behind his purple ear. "I mined the design from the library. I refined it some, and put the components together. Is that building it?"

"Good enough for me. All my projects have been virtual."

The elevator door opened, spilling more light onto the wide balcony. A woman started to step off the elevator, but she hesitated, staring at Skye in surprise. She had creamy skin and red hair in complicated braids that lay flat against her head. She was slender, and at least three inches shorter than Skye. Her eyes looked like Devi's, green flecked with gold, and very pretty when she finally remembered to smile. "Divine, I didn't know you'd invited a friend," she said, stepping out of the elevator at last.

"We were just going out, Mother."

Divine? Skye turned to stare at Devi. Beneath his golden skin his cheeks had flushed a rosy hue.

"Mother, this is Skye—"

"Yes," Devi's mother said. "I recognize her."

Skye frowned, resenting the way real people could link to the city library and withdraw any information they might need at a moment's notice. They could do this because every real person had an atrium—an artificial organ that grew in tendrils throughout their brains. Atriums were biomechanical tissue, capable of receiving and sending subtle radio communications—and of translating those communications into words or pictures or smell or even a sense of touch. When Devi's mother had looked at Skye, she had probably captured Skye's image, sent it to the city library with a request for identification, and received an answer, all in less than a second and in perfect silence.

Ados were not permitted to have atriums, and so they had to rely on fallible memories. It was a rule Skye resented, but she could not hold it against Devi's mother, not in the face of her warm smile.

"Hello, Skye. I'm Siva Hand." She extended her hand and Skye shook it. "Say hello to Yulyssa for me, will you? I haven't seen her in ages."

"I will, ma'am."

Next Siva turned to Devi. "Divine, you won't be out too late?"

"No, Mother."

"You need to practice the sitar."

"Yes, I know."

"I'm glad to see you going out with your friends. Well . . . good night."

The elevator car had waited for them. Skye hurried aboard, turning in time to see Siva Hand at the apartment door, gazing wistfully at Devi as he followed Skye onto the elevator.

The doors started to close. Ord slipped in just before they sealed. Jem hissed, and Devi took a startled step back. "What's that?"

Skye held out her hand so the little robot could climb aboard. "My dokey, I guess. Its name is Ord."

The elevator began its descent, dropping at stomach-jolting speed, like a jump off the column except the sensation lasted only a second.

An awkward silence came over them. Might as well talk about it, Skye thought. Get it over with. So, staring straight ahead and stifling a giggle, she said, "Divine?"

Devi groaned. "Don't ask."

Skye wasn't good at following instructions. "Divine *Hand*?"

"Cute, isn't it?"

Shut up, she told herself. *Shut up. It's not your business.* But she really was bad at following instructions. "You're sixteen, Devi. You could change it."

"You don't know my mother."

"Oh." Siva had seemed very nice. "She must think a lot of you."

"You don't know the half. So who's this Yulyssa my mother mentioned?"

"Oh, you must know her. Yulyssa DeSearange? The mediot? She does the news almost every day. I live with her."

"Oh, right. She's a founder too."

Founders were the original citizens of the city, who had emigrated to Silk 272 years ago. They had arrived to find the city strewn with the bones of the people who had built it, all of them dead of a mysterious plague spawned in Deception Well. Only in the last twenty years had city authority begun to understand the plague. Before then, no one had been allowed down to the planet for fear of contracting the disease. Now anyone could visit, though only on closely supervised tours. There were two small settlements on the coast where a group of scientists and engineers lived full-time, but only a few elite explorers were allowed to mount expeditions into new territory.

The elevator reached the bottom floor and opened. "I'm fourteen now," Skye said as they walked through the lobby. "But I'm not ready to live in Ado Town. I like living with Yulyssa. I had other guardians, but I never got along with them . . . I guess I was a little angry then. Yulyssa is different. She's one of the oldest people in the city, you know. Old enough to let me be myself."

Devi looked uncomfortable. "I wish I could say the same about my mother."

The lobby doors opened and they stepped outside onto a path that glowed with a soft white light. Devi paused to scan the sky. Skye followed his gaze. Only a few stars could be seen through the milky glow of the nebula. "Are you hungry?" she asked. "We could get something to eat."

"Oh. I guess so. I mean, sure. Where——?"

"Message, Skye," Ord interrupted. It rode on her shoulder, so its silky voice spoke directly in her ear. "A message from Zia."

Devi's dokey glared at Ord, growling at the robot's artificial voice.

Skye too felt annoyed at the interruption, but at the same time she also felt strangely relieved. "So play it."

"Hey ado," Ord said, precisely imitating Zia's voice. "So I guess you went to see M. Hand after all. Meet me at the Subtle Virus when you get free, okay? I want to know what M. Hand said, helpful or not. And don't get moody on me if the news was bad. If you don't show up, I'm going to sneak into Yulyssa's apartment and lock a gutter doggie in your breather."

"Wow," Skye said. "Glad that wasn't personal or anything." Then she laughed at the embarrassed look on Devi's face. "Is the Subtle Virus okay with you?"

Zia ambushed them at an intersection near the restaurant. She slid out of a side street just after they had passed. Then she tapped Skye on the shoulder, making her jump. "Hey. It's just me."

"And that's the problem."

Zia grinned. Then her gaze shifted expectantly to Devi. "Hi."

"Hello." Devi's brown cheeks grew a little flushed.

Skye felt suddenly angry. She didn't want to introduce them . . . but that would look pretty stupid, wouldn't it? So what if Zia was a flirt. It didn't mean anything.

"Zia, this is Devi Hand."

Her eyes got wide. For a few seconds she looked frightened, as if she were imagining him as a real person. Then her grin slowly slid back into place. "You're not real."

"Sorry."

Zia laughed. "Well, I'm not."

A commotion erupted in the street below. Skye turned to look, happy for any distraction.

From where they stood, the street curved down and to the right, diving into a cluster of two story buildings with restaurants on balconies that overlooked the street. Ados ducked and darted aside, some of them laughing, others shouting threats and obscenities. "What is it?" Zia asked. But Skye could see no reason for the furor. Not at first.

Then a black spot no more than a couple of centimeters long shot across the luminous white street, moving almost faster than her eye could track. A moment later she heard the harsh *buzz* of tiny mechanical wings furiously drumming the air. "It's a camera bee."

"Sooth," Zia said.

Devi added, "It looks like it's gone crazy."

The bee darted back and forth above the glowing street, diving recklessly into groups of ados, slipping past their swatting hands, doubling back to buzz their noses, sending some of the more timid youths screaming for cover. Camera bees were handled by remote operators . . . so who was handling this one?

"Look out!" Devi yelped, as the bee darted in their direction, bearing down on them with buzzing wings. Zia shrieked and dove aside, while Devi ducked, a split second before the bee blazed past him, almost grazing his ear.

Jem rose to the defense. Balancing on Devi's shoulder, the dokey stood on its hind legs and growled at the bee, as if challenging it to come back.

It did.

It zipped to a stop, flipped over and darted toward them again— only this time it was aimed at Skye.

She glared at it, silently swearing that she would not be made the butt of any dumb ado joke. No one was going to laugh at her for jumping out of the way.

As the camera bee bore down on her, Skye stood her ground.

Zia was picking herself up from the luminous street. "Oh no," she muttered. "You're not playing chicken?"

Ord was getting nervous too. "Bad thing, Skye," it murmured. "Leave. Leave now. Please Skye?"

She didn't answer. Ord stopped talking too. It crouched on her shoulder, perfectly still as the bee zoomed down on them. Then, a moment before it should have hit her or darted aside, Ord's tentacle shot into its path . . . and the bee disappeared, the buzz of its wings instantly silenced.

Skye flinched. Had Ord whacked it out of the air? She looked down, expecting to see it skittering across the ground, but there was no sign of it. "Where . . . ?"

Ord unrolled its tentacle, and the thumb-sized bee tumbled to the illuminated street, its wings motionless, and probably broken.

Jem leaped off Devi's shoulder to sniff and growl at the little machine. Nudging the dokey aside, Devi leaned down to pick up the camera bee. He held it up to his eye. "If we get the ID number, we can find out who it belongs to."

Watching him, Skye had a sudden urge to laugh. "It would be pretty funny if the camera was still on."

Devi's eyebrows rose. "Say hi," he suggested, shoving it in her face. She shrieked and slapped his hand away—

—just as a deep voice boomed up the street. "Hey, Skye!"

Her eyes widened. She whirled around, telling herself it was not him. It couldn't be. Not Buyu. She'd already had the misfortune of running into him once today. She couldn't have crossed paths with him again. Not twice in one day.

But a single glance down the street was enough to assure her that this was indeed the worst of days, for there was Buyu, forcing his ungraceful way through the crowd, receiving many hearty pats on the back—along with a few dirty looks—as he passed. "Skye!" he called again. "Sorry about the camera bee. I was doing some stunts with it, but it got out of control."

"Buyu," Zia sniffed. "So it was *him*."

Ord saw him coming too, and hissed. Skye had never seen the little robot flee anything before, but it picked that moment to slip off her shoulder.

Apparently, Jem had been waiting for just such an opportunity. As soon as Ord touched the ground, the purple and gold dokey launched itself at the robot.

"Look out!" Skye yelled, as the dokey landed on Ord's head.

Jem's fox-like muzzle darted down, biting a chunk of tissue

from the base of one of Ord's tentacles. Zia yelped. Devi roared, "Jem! Stop it. Stop it!"

The startled dokey sprang to the right. Ord saw its chance, and streaked to the left, but as soon as the golden robot moved, the dokey darted after it. Skye yelled and dove for Jem, trying to grab him, but the dokey was too low to the ground, or she was too tall. All she got was a pinch of the loose skin and silky fur behind his neck before Jem slid free.

Skye stumbled after him, off-balance and almost falling down, suddenly aware of Buyu only a step away. She watched him reach down to snatch Ord up with hands as fast as anything she had ever seen.

Then, triumphantly holding the little robot in two hands, far above the reach of the frustrated dokey, Buyu whirled around—

—and Skye crashed into his upraised elbow.

A hot, black explosion of pain clouded her awareness. The next thing she knew, she was sitting on the gleaming street, leaning forward with her hand pressed against her nose while blood dripped out between her fingers. Apparently Ord had once again escaped Buyu, because the little robot was on the ground beside her, one tentacle patting her cheek, the other tapping at the drops of blood glowing a bright ruby red against the light of the street. "Poor Skye. So sad. Nasty, nasty accident. It will fix, Skye."

Then suddenly everybody was all over her with the poor-Skye routine. Zia crouched beside her. "Poor Skye. You never were too graceful. Let's get a look at that nose."

"You okay?" Devi muttered. He scowled at the bright blood droplets in the street, as if he'd never seen blood before. Or maybe he just hadn't seen that much blood before.

Buyu sat down beside her with a thud. His wide, round face looked devastated. "Skye, I'm sorry. I'm just a clumsy fool. I—"

"Itz jus a bloody noz!" she snapped. "It'll figs in a minute."

But blood was still dripping between her fingers. This was crazy. Like everyone else in Silk, her body carried an army of Makers, tiny nanomachines that should quickly repair any trivial wounds.

She'd had a bloody nose before, but it hadn't bled for more than a second or two.

Devi knelt in front of her. Jem was once again perched on his shoulder, and once again he was suspiciously eyeing Ord. Skye shifted her leg to block the robot from the dokey's view. "That should have stopped bleeding by now," Devi said, frowning in concern.

"Well i' hazn't! Give i' a minute."

Her nose felt swollen to three times its normal size. So la di da, she must be looking great just now. A big bloody nose and snot mixed in with the blood. She finally let Zia pull her hands away, and instantly her worst suspicions were confirmed. "Yuck! What a mess. Maybe you should wash your face."

"You thig so?"

Ord raised a tentacle to her nose. She heard a hiss, and felt a cool mist. The bleeding stopped almost immediately, but now her nose felt stuffed with jelled blood. *Zeme dust.*

"You okay?" Devi said, as she clambered to her feet.

"Oh sure. Nothig' wrong here."

"I—"

"Don't mind Miss Nasty," Zia told him. "A little water will wash that temper right off. Get us a table, will you? We'll be back in a minute."

Chapter 6

Did you really find him on a dark rooftop?" Zia asked, as she held a wet towel to Skye's face.

Skye snatched the towel away. "Let me do that!"

She sat in a swivel chair, staring at her projection in an image wall mounted above the ready-room's countertop. The bloodstains on her dress had flaked away, ejected by Makers in the fabric, but her nose looked like a rotten plum, just before the fruit flies started hatching out. It might take an hour for her body's Makers to heal the damage. Or it might take longer.

Why had her nose kept bleeding like that? As a kid, she'd earned a bloody nose once or twice, but it had never bled more than a drop or two. She dabbed at her face, determined to think about something else. "I hope Devi waits for us."

"You're worried he'll take off?" Zia asked.

Skye raised an eyebrow. "Considering his introduction to us . . . who could blame him?"

Zia laughed. "Me, for one. I won't apologize for being exciting company."

"He knows a lot about astronomy."

"I guess, if he sells his articles to the newsfeed."

"I think he knows something about my lifeboat."

"He told you that?"

"He just said that we should talk."

Skye dabbed at her nose again, but there was nothing to be done with it. It was as clean as it was going to get, and it would fix when her Makers fixed it. She sighed, feeling sorely tempted to just sit in the ready room for an hour. Instead she tossed the towel into the recycle and got to her feet.

Ord had been hanging spiderlike in a corner of the ceiling. Now it stirred, lowering itself on one stretching tentacle, while it kept a grip on the ceiling with the tentacle's suction cup tip. "Good Skye. All ready? Time to go to the monkey house, yes?"

Skye glared at the robot. She hated going to the medical center and Ord knew it. At the monkey house, the doctors always wanted to know what you were thinking and how you were feeling, as if feeling bad from time to time was a crime. Skye had spent a good part of her childhood in their company. "It's time to eat, Ord, and if you report a simple bloody nose to the monkey house, I'll turn you in to city authority and have you decommissioned."

Zia aimed a playful kick at the robot. "So turn the little creep in, I say. Ord's more trouble than it's worth."

Ord dodged her foot, scuttling across the floor toward Skye, its limbs rattling on the hard tiles. "Poor Skye. Bad news. The monkey house—"

Skye stomped her foot, suddenly terrified Ord *would* report her bloody nose . . . and then she'd have to turn it in, wouldn't she? Because she had said she would. "Just be quiet, Ord! Okay? Don't bother me about the monkey house. I mean it."

Ord whispered, "Please listen, Skye. It's not—"

Zia scooped up the robot. Before it could melt out of her hands she lobbed it back up into the ceiling corner where it stuck, looking like shiny putty. "Hang out there for awhile, Ord.

Okay?" Then she jerked Skye's arm and they darted laughing out the door.

Of course when Skye glanced back, the robot was already sliding down the wall.

———

As they made their way through the crowd at the Subtle Virus, Skye held her head high, handing out dirty looks to anyone who seemed even a little inclined to comment on the condition of her nose.

She breathed a sigh of relief when she finally spotted Devi waving to catch their attention. He had found a table in a quiet alcove—not an easy accomplishment, given the noise level in the tavern. He stood up, and she saw that his purple dokey had fallen asleep on his shoulder. "Are you all right?" he asked.

"Sure."

Skye took a seat in the U-shaped booth while Devi turned expectantly to Zia. She gave him a coy smile. "Where are you going to sit?" she asked.

Devi looked perplexed. "Oh. I don't know. Here, I guess." He sat down next to Skye. Jem still slept, his monkey paws clasping the fabric of Devi's shirt.

Zia smiled sweetly. "Good. And I'll sit next to you."

Skye rolled her eyes. The Virus might be subtle, but Zia was not. Skye had to scoot all the way around to the other side of the table. Devi followed after her, while Zia sat on his other side.

"I . . . never saw anybody bleed like that," Devi said. "You're sure you—"

"I'm fine," Skye insisted.

Zia added, "She's not from around here, you know."

Skye hadn't thought about that. It was true that people from different worlds really could be different under the skin. Centuries of genetic engineering had produced people who could breathe under water, people who had flexible bones, people who were adapted to frozen worlds, people whose moods oozed onto the air in chemical packets that could change the mood of anyone around them—at least according to city library. In Silk, people were more or less classic human and Skye was no exception. She had never seemed any different from Zia . . . until now.

She told herself it didn't mean anything.

Devi saw it differently. "Maybe you should get the monkey house to check it out, just in case."

"In case of what?" Skye snapped. "I'm fine." She sat up a little straighter, looking around the tavern for a roving chef. "I'm also hungry. Did you order anything yet?"

Devi's expression was suddenly guarded, the way it had been when he was talking to his mother. "No. Buyu went to find his favorite chef."

At the Subtle Virus, the preparation of each meal was a work of art, performed for all the guests to see, and the chefs vied with one another to earn the greatest acclaim—but Skye was more concerned with Devi's reaction than with which chef might serve them . . . until she realized what he had said. "Buyu's here?" she blurted in surprise.

Devi didn't need to answer, because Buyu's voice boomed out from behind her. "Hey Skye, are you okay?"

He dropped onto the only empty space on the U-shaped bench, which of course was right beside her. He leaned over to gawk at her face, until she felt a flush rising up her neck. "Buyu, quit staring at me!"

"I'm sorry, Skye." His voice was softer than she had ever heard it before. As he looked down at the table the bell on the end of his nose ring tinkled, but somehow it wasn't funny anymore. *Buyu was sad.* Skye stared at him for several seconds, shocked at this conclusion. She didn't think she'd ever seen him sad before.

She was pretty sure she didn't like it. She would have to be nice to him, wouldn't she? If he was sad.

"I'm fine," she said yet again, putting on her best smile. "I'm organic. I heal. At least if I'm fed. Did you find a chef?"

"Carlisle's coming to our table—" He held up his hand to stifle her objection. "He's expensive, I know, but only because he's the best chef in the Subtle Virus. Don't worry. I'm paying for it. It's just a way to say I'm sorry."

"You already said that," Zia pointed out. "Then again, I've been hearing about Carlisle for weeks."

A roar went up at the door, loud enough to wake Jem. The dokey raised its head, blinking and yawning. Skye looked too, to see a buoyant crowd pushing into the tavern, bearing two ado boys on their shoulders. Both were well-grown and fully muscled; they might have been anywhere from twenty to a hundred years old. Amid cheers of congratulations, they were set on their feet in the middle of the restaurant. A central table was rapidly cleared. When the two took their seats a wall of admirers closed in around them, and Skye could see nothing more.

"Who are they?" Zia asked.

Buyu answered. "The last two citizens picked for Captain Naveh's planetary expedition."

Skye felt a hollow spot open up deep inside. "Buyu, that's what you wanted to do."

He shrugged. Obviously he had not been picked. He didn't complain about it, though. He didn't say a word.

"Next time that'll be you celebrating," Skye said.

Devi shook his head. His eyes were hard and bright with anger. Jem caught his mood, growling softly deep in his throat. "Don't count on it," Devi said. "We're the last in line for everything. Almost everybody is older than we are, and that means they're more experienced, more knowledgeable, better trained—and with better connections."

"It was a fair competition," Buyu said. "I just didn't score as well."

Devi's anger only deepened as he glared at the raucous crowd. "I'll bet they're almost real. Ninety-eight, at least."

"You can't know that," Zia said.

Ord chose that moment to reappear. Its gold tentacle slid onto the table top. The tip flattened in a suction grip, the tentacle contracted, and Ord's little round head appeared over the table's outer edge. Jem leaped onto the table top, but Devi's hand immediately landed on the dokey's back. "No, Jem."

Ord eyed the dokey. Then it turned its blank gaze on Skye. "Please listen, Skye," it whispered. "Please listen. Bad news—"

"Ord," Zia interrupted. "See those two ados at the central table. The ones talking to— Hey, that's Carlisle!"

The crowd had opened up as an ado in an apron and a chef's red-stenciled headband pushed a cart up to the table. Skye studied him. So this was the famous Carlisle.

Buyu chuckled softly. Almost grimly. "I guess we wait."

Zia's smile had gone away. Leaning close to Ord, she nodded at the central table. "Those two ados, Ord. Check city library. Tell us how old they are."

Ord's head spun briefly around, to follow Zia's gaze. Then the robot slid all the way onto the table top while Devi held onto Jem. "98.6 years and 99.1 years."

Devi nodded in satisfaction. "I told you. Buyu, by the time you get on an exploration team, there won't be a square centimeter of the planet that hasn't been tromped through and analyzed."

"Don't tell him that!" Zia said as she shoved Ord back off the table with a firm hand. "He's got a chance. Everybody's got a chance. Buyu trains hard."

Buyu shook his head, setting his nose bell tinkling. "I'm not good enough. You saw how I messed up with that camera bee. I was using a touch screen to guide it, but my hands are too big and heavy. It got away from me."

"So use a pen," Zia said. Jem craned his neck as Ord slipped a suction-tipped tentacle back onto the table. Zia pried it off, and the little robot disappeared again over the edge.

Devi pulled the dokey into his lap. "The point is, we have to wait a hundred years for anything worth having. I've been trying to get telescope time for two years, but my projects are always turned down, while less original work is accepted, because it's written by someone who's real . . . or almost real."

Skye frowned. "So you're saying there's no way I'll ever get to use the radar system." She felt Ord's gentle *tap-tap* at her ankles, and nudged the robot away.

Devi's smile was slow and cool. Skye wasn't sure she liked it. "No. For you it's just the opposite—"

He looked up in irritation as the restaurant's hostess stopped at the table. She smiled regretfully. "Carlisle sends his apologies. He's obliged to entertain at another table tonight—"

"So we saw," Zia muttered.

"—but another chef will be along shortly. We hope that's all right?"

Buyu shrugged. "We'll get by. Thank you."

When the hostess was gone, Devi immediately resumed his explanation, while he stroked Jem's back with his right hand. "Skye, your circumstances are absolutely unique. And if there really are other lifeboats, then it's also a matter of life and death. If you present your ideas in the right light and then make enough noise, there's no way the project can be turned down. It might be handed over to someone real, but it will still happen, and you'll still be involved."

Skye felt a flush in her cheeks. "So . . . you really think there's a chance other lifeboats are out there?"

"Sure." He put the dokey back onto his shoulder, then slipped a scroll out of his thigh pocket. The shimmery white cloth hardened when he stroked it. He produced a pen, and started jabbing at icons with its blunt tip. "The point is, you'll need to convince top scientists like Tannasen, and that might not be easy." His gaze darted from Skye to Buyu to Zia, including everyone in the conversation. "Think about it. If Skye's great ship was under attack by a Chenzeme warship, it's fair to ask, how many lifeboats might have gotten away? Two or two thousand?"

"We can't know," Skye said, "because there aren't any records. The lifeboat's Dull Intelligence might have known, but it shut down even before Tannasen came, and no one's been able to wake it up again."

As she spoke, Ord's tentacle reappeared on the table. It contracted, and Ord's head rose into sight, just high enough that its optical disks could peer over the table top. Jem tensed, but didn't move.

"Sooth," Devi said. "We can't know, but we can guess. There aren't many records of encounters like that, but in the few we have, no one got away. The Chenzeme warship destroyed them all. We only know what happened because the dying ship sent out a radio message that was intercepted, sometimes years later."

Buyu scowled. "How do you know so much about this?"

"I've studied the subject before."

Skye looked at him in surprise. "You have? Why?"

Devi gave her an odd look, as if he couldn't understand why she would ask such an obvious question. "It's interesting."

"Interesting or not," Zia said—she paused to rap at Ord's tentacle, and Ord immediately disappeared under the table again—"that kind of fact is not going to help our case."

Skye too, didn't like what she was hearing. Could city authority be right? Might she be the lucky exception? She didn't want to believe it. "I'm here," she said. "I got away. That means things went differently when my ship was attacked. My people reacted differently. Maybe they distracted the Chenzeme ship. Or maybe they released the lifeboats when they first saw the warship, long before it got close enough to detect them."

Devi looked pleased. "Sooth. It's what I would have done. The warship might have pursued them for a year or more, before it got close enough to fire its guns. If they knew they couldn't get away, they would have had a year to drop the lifeboats. They might have used the whole year too, dropping them one by one, aiming every lifeboat at Deception Well."

Skye tried to imagine it: for months on end the Chenzeme vessel might have been no more than a faint white gleam in the great ship's telescopes, yet it represented inevitable death bearing down on her family, her people. No human ship could hope to match Chenzeme guns. She looked at Devi. "If the lifeboats were dropped at different times, they might arrive here years apart."

"It seems likely, doesn't it? I mean, you might have been in cold sleep for hundreds of years according to the report I read. That's a lot of time. A small difference in speed could make for a big difference in arrival time."

Buyu looked skeptical. "Skye's been here for years. If there were other lifeboats, someone would have seen their solar sails by now. That's how Skye was spotted."

"No one has seen another sail," Devi said.

The table creaked as Buyu leaned on it. "Which means there aren't any other boats."

"None that have grown sails anyway," Devi responded.

Skye thought about it. "It's possible the nanotech failed. Maybe from cosmic radiation?"

Zia nodded. "Or the DIs might have gotten old and forgotten to activate the nanotech. A dull intelligence doesn't last forever."

Devi nodded. "I think it's possible, even likely, that there are other lifeboats out there somewhere, which have failed to sprout solar sails, for whatever reason. If so, they might be caught in long, elliptical orbits, like comets. They might have already swung around Kheth, only to fall back out through the nebula."

"That would make them hard to find," Zia said. "There's a lot of space out there."

Devi leaned on a fist, looking thoughtful. "Still, it could be done. It *has* to be done. It's so dangerous out there, with the Chenzeme ships always hunting us. Who will look out for us? Who? If we don't look out for each other?"

Ord slipped back onto the table. Devi placed a hand on his dokey, while Zia tried to shove Ord off again. But Ord surprised them all by scuttling toward Buyu—as if that were a zone of safety! As it moved it murmured, "Skye should *not* go to the monkey house. No, no, no. No fun. Skye should listen though. Listen Skye? There is evidence of plague structures in Skye's blood. Skye? This is not good."

Stony silence fell around the table. Skye felt her mouth open. She closed it. Fear was a dry pain in her throat. Across the table, Zia stared at her, wide-eyed with dread. Devi's cheeks had gone sallow beneath his brown skin. Buyu cleared his throat. "Skye—"

"No, wait." She held her hand up to stop him. To stop anyone from saying anything as a chef finally approached their table, pushing a cart full of fruits and pastes and protein cakes. On one end of the cart there was a cutting board, and a small flame that burned under a wok. Skye could smell heated oil.

This chef was an ado girl with thick dark hair that reached her shoulders, and a winning smile. "What would everyone like tonight?" she asked.

Buyu looked at her with a dazed expression. "I think we need a little more time."

"Oh."

Skye stroked Ord's smooth, warm body until they were alone again. "Thank you for waiting, Ord."

"Good Skye."

"I will listen now."

"Yes, good Skye."

"Tell me exactly what you found."

Chapter 7

*P*uzzle pieces," Ord said. It spoke softly, so that its words could not be heard by anyone beyond the table. "City library gives this name to the structures in Skye's blood. It is from an article written 678 years ago, by Liang and Aferra. It is rated 93% plausible, which is a very high plausibility, and has been accessed two times since—"

"Ord," Skye whispered. "What are puzzle pieces?"

Ord's little brow wrinkled, as if it were searching for just the right explanation. "They are incomplete versions of a Chenzeme plague called Compassion."

"That's a strange name for a plague," Buyu said, keeping his voice low.

Zia gave him a hard look. "Let Ord talk."

The little robot crouched perfectly still upon the table, one tentacle tip resting lightly on the back of Skye's hand. In its stillness it looked like a machine, and not at all like the little human she pretended it to be. She listened.

"Liang and Aferra record the outbreak of an unknown plague in a city called Nanda Wes on a newly colonized frontier world. All adults in the city died of this plague when their Makers failed to overcome the infection. The children survived. The plague did not attack the children. Nanda Wes was quarantined, and the children were carefully tested. No sign of the plague could be found in their tissues, so compassionate rescuers removed them from the city. They were taken in by adoptive families all over the frontier world. Then, within a few weeks, new outbreaks of Compassion occurred. Each outbreak began in a family that had adopted an older child from Nanda Wes—except this time the child died too. All of these children were at the end of their growing period."

"In other words," Devi said, "physically they had become adults."

Ord bobbed its little head. "Sooth. In time it became clear that children were carriers of Compassion. The DNA in every human cell is a chemical code that instructs the body how to grow. Most of this code is dormant. Only a few parts of the DNA are active at any time. Compassion used this fact to hide itself. In the children's DNA it hid the instructions for building itself. Not all in one location, where it might be easy to find. Instead, it broke the instructions into small groups of code, and scattered these throughout the children's DNA. These tiny, scattered parts went undetected by those who rescued the children of Nanda Wes."

"So when the kids grew up," Devi said, "the dormant plague rebuilt itself . . . and killed them?"

"Sooth." Ord patted Skye's hand with its soft, warm tentacle. "It also spread to the compassionate adults who had adopted the orphaned children, and killed many millions of them. It is called Compassion, because it exploits the natural love any adult will feel for a helpless child."

"That's evil!" Zia squeaked, trying to keep her outrage at low volume.

She glanced around nervously, while Ord bobbed its head again. "Sooth. Smart Zia is right. It is a clever, evil Chenzeme plague."

Many Chenzeme plagues were known, and almost all of them were spread through animate microscopic dust. *Zeme dust.* Skye's skin felt cold, and her hand trembled under Ord's tentacle. "So Ord, you're saying I have this plague called Compassion embedded in *my* DNA?"

Ord's little mouth puckered up, as if this were a difficult question to answer. "That is the logical conclusion to draw from the presence of puzzle pieces in your blood."

"But I don't feel sick!" Skye whispered. "I am *not* dying."

Ord's tentacle *tap-tapped* against her hand. "Yes. Skye is clever and strong. Skye is fine. Sooth. For now."

"For now? Come on, Ord. Explain it all. What's the meaning of these puzzle pieces?"

Ord's tentacle trembled for just a second. "In the article, Liang and Aferra surmise that as growth hormones decline, the alien DNA gradually becomes active. At first only parts of the plague structure are built. These are 'puzzle pieces.' They are harmless."

"Like a model with missing parts," Devi said.

"Yes. As growth hormones continue to decline, all parts of the alien DNA become active. The plague structure is fully formed, and now it is harmful, and contagious. For a day, maybe two, there will be no sign of illness as the plague is spread from adult to adult. Then it kills."

Skye didn't want to ask how it killed. "And it's these puzzle pieces that you've found in my blood." Harbingers of the disease to come. "How much time do I have before the plague becomes active?"

Zia's cheeks glistened with perspiration. Her voice sounded a note too high as she said, "Skye, the monkey house can cure this! Ord's article is six hundred years old. There's a cure by now. Right, Ord?"

"So sorry, no," Ord said. "Not yet." It sank down against the table, almost puddling. "The monkey house is very clever, good Skye. Not fun, no. Just very clever."

Skye slipped her hand out from under Ord's tentacle. She rubbed at her cheeks. Her skin felt cold and clammy. Her heart did too. "Ord, if it's only puzzle pieces then the plague's not active yet. No one else could have caught it from me, right?"

Once again Ord bobbed its head. "Yes, if Liang and Aferra are correct."

"And there's no one in Silk I could have caught it from."

"This plague structure is not known here," Ord confirmed.

"So I brought it with me from the great ship. That's what you're saying?"

"Unknown, Skye. City library does not say."

"How long before this plague becomes active?" she asked again.

Everyone huddled together, awaiting Ord's answer. "Liang and Aferra propose seven to ten days," Ord said.

Zia made a little moan deep in her throat. "Skye—"

"I don't think I'm hungry," Skye said. Her voice had an ugly squeak to it. She started to get up, but she was trapped in the booth by Buyu.

He stared at her, his eyes glistening with too much moisture. "This is crap, Skye," he whispered. "It's unprocessed garbage. Ord doesn't know what it's talking about. There's nothing wrong with you."

Skye looked up, startled to see that the hostess of the Subtle Virus had returned to their table. Had she overheard anything? Surely not. Yet she frowned suspiciously at Buyu. "Ah . . . are you all ready for dinner yet?"

"No," Devi said. His voice was curt. "Something's come up. We won't be having dinner tonight. Thank you. Thank you." He scooted against Zia, bumping her out of the booth.

"Hey—!" she protested as she stumbled to her feet.

"Are you quite certain?" the hostess asked. She looked seriously annoyed. Skye was glad to see it, sure now that she had not overhead any talk of plague. "The special tonight is grilled fungus with synchovy stuffing."

"Another time," Devi growled as he stood up behind Zia.

Skye watched him anxiously, waiting for him to run away, to alert the monkey house. And why shouldn't he? *I would.* Seven to ten days. She suddenly felt terribly small, and horribly alone.

But Devi didn't leave. He was standing by the table, glaring at her with a fierce expression. "Come on!" he commanded.

"W-what?" she stammered. "Where?"

"Out of here. Some place private. Where we can talk."

She blinked at him, not getting it. "You want to talk to me?"

Devi rolled his eyes. "Skye? Please?"

The hostess treated him to a disapproving frown. "If the lady would like to stay—"

"No," Buyu said, scooting out from his seat. "She's coming with us." He turned, and very deliberately, he held out his hand to her. "Come on, Skye. You're not as scary as you like to think."

———

Outside, the night sky gleamed faintly white with the light of the nebula. Only a handful of bold stars shone through it. Skye felt herself gliding dreamlike on the gleaming street. Sounds arrived muffled as if by distance and her skin felt numb. Inside, though, deep in her core, her sense of self blazed hot and frightened and vitally alive.

Seven to ten days. Worlds had changed in far less time than that.

"You shouldn't be with me," she said abruptly. She looked around. Devi was just ahead, rushing down the street like a madman, almost breaking into a run on the steeper sections, turning back every few steps to exhort her to "Hurry up!" Jem held onto his shoulder, an awestruck expression on his little fox face as if he had never traveled so quickly before. Zia held onto Skye's elbow, almost as crazy for speed as Devi. Buyu followed a step behind.

"You shouldn't be with me," Skye repeated, stumbling to a stop in the middle of the street. "At the least, it will mean trouble from city authority when they find out what's—"

Zia gave her elbow a little shake. "Shut up. Devi's got something in mind and I don't think it's the monkey house."

"We can't talk here," Devi growled. "Just come on, Skye. Trust me, okay?"

She wondered why she should. She had only just met him. But strangely enough, it was easy to nod and say, "Okay."

They followed the street all the way down to the base of the city, where it merged with the broad promenade that bordered

Splendid Peace Park. Splendid Peace was a huge greenway that ran all the way around the city's circular base. The park promenade separated the woodland from the city's residential slopes. Devi darted across it, startling several real people who were out for an evening stroll. Skye heard gasps, and two or three mutters that sounded like *crazy ados*.

At those half-imagined words, a rich, luscious sense welled up in her, a bright consciousness of being alive, crazy wild alive, full of life that was as sweet as night-blooming flowers, intoxicating as music tuned to your mood. She let this giddy sense fill her, until it bubbled out of her mouth in a merry laugh.

Devi turned to look at her with a quizzical gaze.

"Come on," she urged him in return. "Hurry!" And she sprinted past him, tagging him on the side as she went. Behind her Zia shouted, and Buyu called out in surprise, but Skye didn't slow down. She dashed into the park, her filmy skirt waving behind her like a fin.

She followed a narrow, luminescent foot trail that led her away from the promenade and into the darkness that huddled under the spreading branches of the trees. She could hear Devi running a step behind. She had no idea where they were going—where he intended them to go—but in that moment she knew where she wanted to be . . . in the most isolated, awesome place in the whole city.

She raced along the foot trail, startling the occasional couple clutching in the shadows, and every time the trail branched, she took the fork that led deeper into the park, until, within a few minutes, the city's lights were all but lost behind the vegetation. Her breath tore in and out of her lungs, sweat poured from her cheeks, and her belly felt slack with hunger, but she didn't slow. If she could run fast enough, she could run away from fear. She knew she could.

A few minutes later the path came to an end. It flowed into a shimmering pond of light—a gleaming pavilion only a couple of meters wide. Being afraid was part of being alive, wasn't it? She edged across the pavilion. Her shoulders heaved as she drew in great lungfuls of air bearing the scent of flowers and mulch, the sound of night insects. Shrubs crowded the pavilion on all sides but one. She crept up to that open space. This was where the world ended.

The city of Silk was like a conical bead hung on the column of the elevator cable, enclosed by a transparent canopy that kept the air in. Here at the base of the city, along the outside edge of Splendid Peace Park, the canopy reached all the way to the ground.

Skye eased forward until her toes reached the very edge of the pavilion, and then she looked past her toes . . . at nothing. Or rather, at a great empty ocean of space unfolding before her.

Her heartbeat had begun to slow, but now it picked up again. She breathed a little faster. If she raised her hand, if she moved her toes just a little farther, she would feel the canopy's transparent membrane, and the effect would be shattered. But for now it felt as if she stood on the edge of the world, on the edge of life, with the Universe spread out beneath her feet and if she took but one step more she would plunge into it.

The dark mass of the planet loomed below her. Tiny sparks of lightning could be seen flickering in some distant thunder storm. Beyond the planet lay the thready white gleam of the nebula where uncountable numbers of butterfly gnomes lived their silent lives, and beyond that the bright stars whose names she didn't know, and the Chenzeme ships prowling menacingly between them, and beyond that . . . Well, beyond the nearest stars lay *everything*—all the other stars and dust clouds and black holes of the galaxy, and distant galaxies beyond that, and galactic clusters, and quasars, their light almost as old as the Universe itself. And time. Looking at ancient starlight was like looking back in time.

Skye smiled, filled with reverent wonder. No wonder Devi had fallen in love with astronomy. In the night, everything can be seen.

She was suddenly aware of Devi standing beside her, so close the heat of his body touched hers. The slowing pace of his breath was like the city breathing. "They're out there somewhere," he said, his voice low.

"Who?" Her own voice no more than a whisper.

"Your people. The other children from the great ship. Do you see? We had it all wrong. There was no Chenzeme warship. Your parents . . . they must have put you in the lifeboat to protect you from Compassion plague. They might have been like the rescuers at Nanda Wes. They might have thought that you—that all the children—had a resistance to the plague. So they put you aboard lifeboats, and sent you toward Deception Well, hoping that a compassionate people would find you, and raise you, after they were gone."

Had it been that way? She glanced at him. Jem still balanced on his shoulder, though the little dokey looked frightened. His claws dug into Devi's shirt and his tail swished. Devi absently stroked Jem's chest. Sweat glistened on his cheeks as he stared into the abyss.

Skye said, "So there could be hundreds, thousands of other children out there. Every child from the great ship. Why haven't we seen them? Why haven't we seen their solar sails?"

"I don't know. It's a mystery. There may be some clue aboard the lifeboat."

She shook her head. The lifeboat was far away. "Nothing was ever found. Whatever records it once carried were hidden or erased."

"Still, other lifeboats have to be out there. If it wasn't a Chenzeme warship . . ."

Skye reached up to stroke Jem's soft fur. "If it wasn't a warship, then every lifeboat should have survived. But Devi, everyone of them will be a plague carrier . . . like me."

He turned to her and nodded grimly. Jem took that moment to scamper down his arm and drop to the ground. The dokey's claws clicked against the pavilion as it paced, sniffing at the night air. Devi watched his pet for a few seconds. Then he leaned against the invisible wall, and slid down until he was sitting halfway over nothing. "Ord's right, you know. The monkey house might cure it. The trouble is—"

"I know. Or, I think I can guess. If the doctors can't cure it—"

"Everyone of those kids is doomed. City authority won't pick them up if they're plague carriers."

Skye sat down beside him, smoothing her skirt over her knees. The elation she had felt was still with her, but quieter now, like a stream that has left the rapids to flow unruffled over smooth, round stones and past the bright orange scales of koi fish. "You're not afraid of me."

"I'm afraid *for* you." Devi's voice was low and rough. "There's a third thing that could happen."

Jem came over, and she stroked the dokey's soft fur. "Tell me."

"If the monkey house can't cure you, the doctors still might find a way to control the plague by controlling your metabolism— never letting you grow quite all the way up."

"You mean they could use medical Makers to undo all my body's growing." She shuddered. It would be like an artist every night deleting all the colors that had been summoned that day into her painting, every night erasing a fresh layer of meaning from her life's work. Skye gazed at the palm of her hand. "This is all that's left of my mother and father. I don't want to change it. Not now. Not like this."

She looked up, as muttered obscenities and the sound of approaching footsteps arrived from the forest trail. A moment later she heard the low buzz of a hunting camera bee . . . and for the first time realized that Zia and Buyu were missing. She smiled. Then she leaned back against the invisible wall, and it was as if she were leaning against the Universe itself.

From somewhere nearby Zia called, "*Sky-eye! Where are you?*"

Softly Skye said, "City authority would never let me out of the monkey house if I was a carrier. No matter what. Would they? And they would not pick up the other children, if they could not be cured."

"So that leaves only one option," Devi said as the camera bee buzzed into sight, a faint gold spark emerging from the darkness under the trees. Devi waved at it. "Hey Buyu, we're here." Then he turned to Skye. "We have to see to it you're cured."

Skye laughed softly. "Sooth. I'll go for that."

Zia burst into the clearing, her hair a mess, and her eyes looking wide and wild in the upwelling light. "Say that again, ado."

"Say what?" Skye asked, as the bee buzzed between them. It bumped against the transparent wall, sputtered a high note, then tumbled to the ground. Jem leaped on it instantly, and picked it up in his teeth.

"What you just said to him. Say it again, only say it louder."

"I'll go for that?"

"Louder, ado. Like you mean it."

"I'll go for that!"

"Slick." She dropped cross-legged to the center of the little gleaming pavilion. Her gaze went to Devi. "Has she stopped being crazy?"

"Do you want her to?"

Zia grinned. "Never."

"I have to go to the monkey house," Skye said.

"Buyu!" Zia shouted. "Where are you?"

"Coming! I'm almost there. I crashed the bee again, didn't I?"

"You did a great job," Zia called. "You found them. Jem's eating the bee, though."

"Gutter-dogs!"

But Devi was already wrestling the device out of the dokey's mouth.

Buyu clattered into the pavilion, still clutching the bee's guidance screen in one hand. "Hey Skye. You okay?"

"Better," she admitted.

"Uh-uh," Zia said. "Too tentative. I want you to say 'I'll-Go-For-That.' I want you to say it loud and clear when Buyu shares with you the most beautifully elegant, yet simple plan you will ever have the pleasure of hearing. Remember now, 'I'll-Go-For-That.' And if you ever call him Buyu-the-brainless again, I will cut off all your hair the next time I catch you asleep. Buyu?"

"She called me brainless?"

"In jest, dear. Tell her now."

Awkwardly, he lowered his bulk to the pavilion floor, sitting between Skye and Zia. The faint light dimmed noticeably, blocked by his large body. He leaned forward, his elbows on his knees. "Ord said seven to ten days, right? So there's time to experiment.

Nobody's going to get hurt if you don't go to the monkey house right away."

"If Ord is right," Devi interjected.

"Oh sooth, but personal DIs like Ord, they just don't get chemistry wrong."

"Go ahead with it," Zia said. Her eyes looked as sharp as Jem's had, a moment before he leaped on the camera bee.

"Right. Well. We're living above one of the strangest planets listed in the library, aren't we?" Buyu asked. "Deception Well. Where nothing is quite what it seems. It's a wilderness, but it's watched over by some of the slickest tech anyone's ever encountered. Remember the governors?"

Devi slapped his thigh. "*Of course!*" He sounded half-angry, half-elated.

"The governors are the microscopic guardians of this place," Buyu went on. "They're a nanotech system left here, 30 million years ago, by the intelligent species that used to call this planet home. They were designed to defend this world . . . against the Chenzeme, we guess. Luckily for us, they don't attack unless they're attacked first . . . otherwise we wouldn't be here talking about it, because we don't have any Makers that can beat them."

Skye nodded. The governors were the reason no warship had ever been seen near Deception Well. Not only were they everywhere on the planet and in the city, but they inhabited the nebula too. She glanced up at the milky filaments shimmering in the night sky. If a warship entered the system, it would be infected by the governors. They would take it apart if it tried to attack.

Buyu stroked the fuzzy line of beard that traced his jawbone. "The Well governors can out-maneuver any nanotech systems the Chenzeme have, too. Even Chenzeme plagues, Skye. Remember city history? You know it's happened before."

"Once," Zia said. "It's happened just once before. When a man named Jupiter Apolinario was dying of a Chenzeme plague he went down to Deception Well, and he was cured. You don't need the monkey house, Skye. You don't need to take a chance with them. Be like Apolinario—go down the Well and let the governors clean that Chenzeme death wish out of your cells."

It sounded crazy. Go down the Well? City authority would never let her go down the Well and hang out—la di da—until she was cured. It was mystic, magic, wishful thinking. Besides, there were microscopic governors everywhere in the city too. If they could cure her, why hadn't they done it already? "I don't think—"

"Ah, ah!" Zia said, pointing an accusing finger. "Remember what the right and proper answer is? You rehearsed it."

"But why go down the Well?"

"That's not the right answer."

"Well then, *how* could I go down the Well?"

Her eyes narrowed. "Take the elevator, ado. What did you think? Tours go down every day."

"Oh sure, but those people have to come right back up."

"Not really," Devi said. "They're down for seven or eight hours."

"Do you think that's long enough . . . ?"

"Probably not," Buyu said. "Apolinario was down there for days."

"And his plague was active," Zia added. "Skye, the fact that you have 'puzzle pieces' is a pretty good sign that the governors don't even recognize your infection as a threat. But you know I've been interning with a planetary biologist, and believe me, Deception Well is a crazy world. With the help of the governors, the biosphere has learned to grow its own libraries. There are hundreds of thousands of communion mounds sprouting from the soil. They're made up of thousands of different organisms, some native, some Chenzeme, some from Earth, all living together as one. Maybe that had a purpose once, though really I think they're just a chaos of smart biology that learned how to get along. The point is, they act like libraries of biological data, especially *human* biological data. If there's already a cure for Compassion in the biosphere of the Well, then we're going to find it in one of those mounds."

Skye felt her pulse quickening in anticipation. Communion mounds were not found in the city, but only in the Well. "We could bring Ord with us. It could sift through a mound, and find the molecular structure we need."

"Exactly. Let the little chemist be useful for once in its pointless existence. Where is it, anyway?"

Skye shrugged. "Around." Ord was always around. That was its deepest instinct.

"Aren't the communion mounds off limits to tourists?" Devi asked.

Zia gave him a dark look. "I said we were taking the elevator down. I didn't say we were going on a regular tour. Regular tourists are escorted by nasty little robot wardens, so that they can't get away with anything. However"—she patted Buyu's knee—"we are lucky enough to have a trained explorer in our midst."

Buyu blushed. Even in the dim light, Skye could see it.

Zia went on with her explanation. "Buyu hasn't been placed on an explorer team yet, but he is allowed to escort small parties down on day trips, so we won't have to take a robot warden along. With any luck, we can tap a mound and city authority will never know the difference."

Skye shook her head. Already she could see a hundred things wrong with the plan—not the least of which was that Buyu would be risking the career he wanted so badly. If it was discovered they were tapping the mounds, Buyu might be permanently suspended from the explorer corps. "It might be all right for me and Ord to try it," Skye said, "but you three—you've got nothing to gain and everything to lose by defying city law."

Zia pouted. "That is not the answer I coached you to say. Try again."

"Sooth, Zia's right," Devi said. "Try it again, because we have a lot to lose too. Skye?"

Buyu nodded. "Don't make me kidnap Ord and go by myself, Skye. Without you, the little guy would melt into a puddle at the bottom of my pack."

She laughed softly.

"Say it," Devi whispered.

"Say it!" Zia commanded, louder.

"Say it," Buyu muttered. "Please Skye?"

Skye closed her eyes, thinking of the thousands of lifeboats that might even now be falling in long slow orbits around Kheth. If there was no cure for this plague, they would be falling forever. She opened her eyes, and looked at her friends, one by one. "You all are crazy! Crazier than me. But okay. If you know how, if you want to do it, then *I'll go for that!* Okay?"

"Slick," Zia said, nodding in satisfaction.

"First elevator down tomorrow," Devi added.

Buyu had already turned to more pressing matters. "We never ate dinner," he moaned. "I'm *starving!*"

Chapter 8

No one was more real than Yulyssa DeSearange. She was the oldest person in the city, and yet she had not let the years harden her thoughts and beliefs. Her eyes and mind were always open to the subtle changes of the world around her. She saw everything, and she could read meaning into every detail. When Skye walked into their apartment, Yulyssa took one look at her and asked, "Are you all right? What's happened?"

She lay half-reclined on the sofa, a small woman of delicate build, several centimeters shorter than Skye. In the evening Yulyssa often lay on the sofa, visiting friends through the atrium in her head. Now she sat up. Her long, black hair slipped like a veil across her finely sculpted cheek. As with any real person, her age did not show in her face or in her body, but only in the weight of her gaze and the calmness of her bearing. Compared to Yulyssa, Skye felt that everything about herself was in a muddle: her health, her hair, her judgment, her dress. "Oh, I—" She searched for something to say. "I'm exhausted. It's been a terribly long day."

Yulyssa's eyes continued to take her measure, but she asked no more questions. "I heard you and Zia set a jump record."

"Sooth. It was a lot harder than I thought it would be."

Ord had slipped into the kitchen. Now it came out with a glass of water for Skye. She drank it gratefully, while Yulyssa made a space on the sofa for her. Skye sat down. "I met a new boy tonight. I've never met anyone like him before."

"Divine Hand," Yulyssa said.

Skye turned to her, furious and frightened to think that Yulyssa had somehow been spying on her. "How do you know that?"

"Siva Hand called me an hour ago. She was in quite a state. Divine had gone out with this wild foreign girl and he hadn't come home when she expected."

"You're not serious."

Yulyssa's smile was deliciously naughty. "Oh I am."

Skye covered her mouth to stifle a giggle. "Poor Devi."

"Don't think too badly of Siva. Like most of us, she lost all her family when the Chenzeme warships wrecked our ancestral world of Heyertori. She never got over it. Not really. We were all refugees when we came to Deception Well. Siva worked as hard as anyone. She denied herself a family for years upon endless years. When she finally retired from public service, it was to have a child. Specifically, it was to have Divine."

Yulyssa shook her head. "It was not a healthy choice. The past is the past. Siva should have let it go, as the rest of us have, and started anew. But she would not. She had Divine made from the genetic record of her first born son, who died with our world of Heyertori. Divine is a genetic clone of that young man. He is a constant reminder to her of what she has lost, and what she still could lose. Even the most logical of us can be haunted by a dread that the past will repeat itself . . . and Siva is not the most logical woman I have ever known."

"So she worries over him all the time," Skye said. How dreadful, to be the stand-in for a dead past. "Doesn't she know that will only drive him away?"

Yulyssa shrugged. "The heart is ruled by its own kind of sense."

"Or nonsense," Skye said. "Did she really call me a wild foreign girl?"

"Yes. Those were the words."

"Actually, that's kind of slick."

Yulyssa nodded, her tongue firmly in her cheek. "I thought so."

Skye kissed her. "I'm going to bed now, before I fall asleep on my feet."

———

Skye was up again before first light. Overnight, the Makers that lived on her skin had cleaned away the day's sweat and oil, so that she woke up clean. Her bed was slightly stained, but a nanodrizzle, looking like a thread of glistening water that never got anything wet, was already flowing over the waste and absorbing it. Within minutes the bed would be clean too.

Moving quickly, Skye first stuffed her skin suit into a cloth sack, then pulled on a blue sweater and gray knickers. She ran her fingers through her short, soft brown hair, then glanced at herself in the image wall. A wild foreign girl, huh? Well, at least her nose had healed.

She went barefoot into the gray, predawn world, while Ord followed in the shadows, the light from the street glinting off its golden hide. Wild canaries were just starting to sing their morning greetings, while a gutter doggie wandered fat and stupid up the street, its sausage-like body bloated with the waste matter it had scavenged in the night. It looked at her with dull eyes, then headed on toward its tunnel, where it would unroll its sponge-like body into a great, flat sheet that it would press against the tunnel walls. The walls would absorb its waste, returning the matter to the city's recycling system.

The streets were empty, the restaurants closed. Skye saw only two ado boys, making their slow way into an apartment building. Judging from their haggard faces, they must have just barely survived a hard night of partying. She hurried on to Shachi Street, then down a short flight of steps into a transit station. An empty car was already waiting on the platform. Its door slipped silently open as she approached. Ord scuttled after her, then reached for her sack with its tentacles, and climbed aboard. Skye dropped onto the seat. "Elevator terminus," she said.

The door slid shut, enclosing her in an airtight capsule. The car accelerated away from the platform, following the track through a white gel membrane that sealed the station from the airless tunnels of the transit system. As soon as the car *shooshed* through the membrane, there was nothing to see, for the transit tunnels were pitch black. Skye could feel the car turning, though, as it shot through the city's industrial interior, making for the core and the elevator column. Only moments later the car slipped through another gel membrane, and once again the clean white light of a transit station spilled through the windows.

Zia and Buyu were already waiting on the platform. Skye waved, then hopped out when the door opened.

"Feeling okay?" Buyu asked, his thick brow wrinkled in dire concern.

Skye was relieved to see that he had removed his nose bell. "Sooth, dweeb. I'm not contagious yet."

"I didn't mean—"

"Buyu? I'm joking." She turned to Zia and they smacked their palms together. "I'm scared."

"And I'm your mother."

Skye grinned. Buyu and Zia were already wearing their skin suits. The garments were required gear planetside, an intelligent hide that would protect the wearer from scrapes and jabs and encounters with unfriendly beasties. Buyu's skin suit was the muddy brown color of the explorer corps. Zia's gold suit gleamed beside it like hot metal.

"You're not dressed," Zia observed.

Skye hefted her cloth sack. Ord's little golden head peeked out of it. "I'm going to change now. I didn't want Yulyssa to know that we were . . . you know. She's so smart. Sometimes I feel like she knows what I'm thinking before I do. I didn't want her to guess. . . . Well, it's silly. I'll go change now."

When she came back, Ord was on the shoulder of her glowing blue skin suit, the sack had been stashed in a locker, and Devi still hadn't arrived. Buyu had bought breakfast though, so the three of them sat on the station stairs, eating, while they watched transit car after transit car arrive at the station. Only a few ados got out. Most of the new arrivals were real people, dressed in skin suits for the journey down to the planet where they had been forbidden to go for most of their lives.

"What if the elevator car fills up?" Skye wondered.

Buyu said, "I reserved four tickets. We'll get on if we're at the gate on time." Then, after a pause, "Maybe Devi changed his mind."

Skye felt a flash of temper, but she bit down on a retort. Hadn't she been thinking the same thing?

"How much time do we have?" Zia asked.

"Couple of minutes."

"Zeme dust."

Skye stared at the white gel membrane that sealed off the transit tunnel, willing another car to come through.

None came.

Apparently, everyone who was going on the dawn tour had already arrived.

Well, Devi was under a lot of pressure at home.

She thought about sharing with Zia the things Yulyssa had told her last night, but she was pretty sure Devi wouldn't like it. He would probably be angry if he knew *she* knew. Maybe he did know. Maybe that's why he hadn't come.

She stood up, then pitched the remains of her breakfast into a recycle slot. "Let's go."

"You don't want to wait just another minute?" Zia asked.

"Why? If he were coming, he'd be here. Something must have come up, but that doesn't mean *we* should miss our ride down— unless you've changed your mind?"

"Knock it off, Skye. You're talking like a dumb ado."

Zia got up and dumped her trash too. Buyu devoured his last bite, then pitched his rubbish and grabbed a pack he'd left lying on the stairs. He hefted it. "Food and a few supplies. We'll be on our own for hours." He grinned, obviously delighted at the thought.

They passed through the gate and into a huge loading bay, its roof lost in shadows far overhead. The elevator car waited behind a transparent wall. Perhaps "car" was the wrong word, for this car was the size of a building nine stories high. Through its tall window walls Skye could see people milling about between rows of benches on the lower floors.

She followed Buyu through an open airlock. A smiling attendant greeted them just inside. Skye was pleased to see that the interior was not nearly so crowded as she had feared. There were a lot of people on the first floor, but an escalator on one side of the huge, open room made it easy to reach the upper levels. Most of the real people were traveling in large groups of long time friends—only a few of them, like Yulyssa, ever seemed to do anything alone—and so they were clustered on the first three floors. Skye, Zia, and Buyu, rode the escalators up, until they found an empty floor. Then for good measure, they went one floor higher.

Rows of benches faced the window wall, but Skye spurned them. She sat cross-legged on the carpet, her knees touching the glass as she looked down at the loading bay. Zia dropped beside her, while Buyu sat on a bench. "Longest jump we'll ever make, hey ado?"

Skye raised her hands. "And look. No tether." She gazed across the loading bay, but she did not see Devi. "I don't feel sick at all."

"Hush. Don't talk about it here."

"Do you think he got scared?"

"Maybe. I'm pretty scared."

"It's funny, 'cause I'm not. Not really."

The lights dimmed. Skye tensed. At the gate she'd been given a radio headset to listen to an information monologue if she wanted, but she'd dropped it on the first bench on her way up. If she had a question about the Well she would ask Buyu or Zia. Otherwise, she just wanted to experience it, to discover it for herself.

She felt herself drop. It was only a brief plummeting sensation, but suddenly the floor of the loading bay rushed up to engulf the window. A fleeting interlude of darkness followed, lasting maybe a second and a half, and then the elevator fell into sunlight. The dizzying speed and the abrupt transition—it *was* like jumping.

Kheth had risen just a few degrees over the rim of the planet. Its slanting rays had barely touched the land below them, but here on the elevator column its light seared. Skye craned her neck to look down upon a cloudless pre-dawn world. The ocean glimmered faint gray, but Deception Well's equatorial continent remained a dark silhouette, its ragged southern edge looking like black fingers raking the water. The elevator rushed toward it with heart-hammering speed.

"Message, Skye. Real time."

She turned to scowl at Ord. It crouched at her knee, its tentacles contracted into stubby limbs. "From who?"

"Devi Hand, no doubt," Zia said.

"Yes. Smart Zia."

"You talk to him," Skye said. She did not want to admit to the disappointment she felt.

"Never mind," Devi called, his voice arriving from the direction of the escalator. "I guess I found you."

Skye twisted around in surprise. Devi was just pulling off the little radio headset each of them had received at the gate. He dropped it on a bench. He wore an olive-green skin suit, with his blond and red hair tied in a neat ponytail behind his neck. Watching him, Skye couldn't decide if she was furious or madly happy. Maybe both.

He studied her in turn, as he made his way past the benches. There was something of dark anger around his eyes, enhanced by the little triangle of red beard on his chin. "Are you still talking to me?"

Skye flushed and turned back to the window. Then she gasped in surprise. Already, they had fallen halfway to the world. She put her hand on the glass. "I thought you weren't coming."

He sat on the bench next to Buyu. "I told you I was coming."

"Sooth."

"I got held up."

"It's what we figured," Buyu said.

That wasn't quite true, but it was nice of him to say it.

Devi added, "I searched all the floors on the elevator car and I didn't see you. Did you know the floor below is empty? When I saw that, I thought *you* had decided not to come. That's when I called."

"I said I was going," Skye answered.

"Sooth."

Below them, the ocean had begun to flush pink with the dawn's light. Skye could just make out a ragged line of forest along the coast.

"I'm moving out of my mother's house," Devi announced.

Skye twisted around to look at him. "Your telescope—"

He shrugged. "There's not much to see from inside this nebula anyway."

She nodded, wondering if it was all her fault.

Chapter 9

During the final five hundred meters of the descent, the elevator car slowed to a crawl, so that it felt as if they were floating down among the trees that clothed the steep sides of a bowl-shaped valley. The elevator terminus was a circular black platform that filled the valley floor, rising thirty meters above the nearest trees. A U-shaped bay formed an opening on one side of the platform. The car descended into it, coming to rest between the wings of the building.

Skye stood up slowly, gazing out the window in amazement. An empty road ran out from the terminal building. It was flanked on either side by two meters of neat lawn, but all signs of civilization ended there. Beyond the manicured grass the forest rose far overhead, a green wall of ancient, crowding trees, their massive branches reaching over the broad roadway to catch what light they could. Skye had never imagined that trees could truly grow so big. She'd seen forests in virtual reality sims, but she had never understood quite so clearly that such giants could be real.

"Buyu, this is so slick." She reached down to scoop up Ord. "Come on, come on. I want to get outside."

———

They embarked onto a wide pavilion, where three explorers in mud-brown skin suits like Buyu's were greeting the incoming tour groups. Most of the groups were being sent up to the roof, where aircraft waited to take them to the two small coastal settlements. As they set off for the escalators, each group was joined by a small, glassy, humanlike figure less than a meter high. These were the wardens. Like Ord, they were biogel robots, but the wardens looked as if they were made of dark green glass, fashioned to resemble some lithe human child, though their faces looked only half-formed. For centuries, wardens had been used to explore the planet's surface. Now they watched over tour groups, monitoring their actions and immediately reporting any violation of the rules.

Skye smiled at a line of five wardens waiting with machine patience at the edge of the pavilion. Let the little spies accompany someone else! Buyu was a trained explorer, and he was all the escort they would need. She boosted Ord up to her shoulder.

"Buyu Mkolu!"

Skye turned to see one of the three resident explorers waving a friendly greeting. She was a tall, muscular woman, with dark blue hair the color of deep water. As she strolled across the pavilion to meet them, it was easy to see by her bearing that she was very real. "Welcome back, Buyu."

Buyu looked shocked to see her. "Hello, Sensei Matilé." He raised his hand to touch palms with her, yet he did not seem able to meet her gaze. He looked very nervous—as if guilt were knocking behind his eyes, trying to get out. Sweat glistened on his cheeks and Skye felt sure it wasn't caused by the steamy tropical air.

Apparently, Matilé too, noticed his distress. Her eyes narrowed as she examined him. "Are you all right?"

"Oh. Sooth." Buyu took a deep breath, then managed to grin

his big, sloppy Buyu-grin. Skye sighed in heartfelt relief. Maybe he wouldn't give them away after all?

Buyu told Sensei Matilé, "This is the first time my friends have been down."

He introduced them, and a few pleasantries were exchanged. Then Matilé said, "You'll have to take a warden with you today."

Again, Buyu lost his composure. "What? Why? Sensei, I've finished my training. I've been cleared for day tours—"

Matilé raised her hand. "Buyu, I know. It's just that everyone must be escorted today. An acid dragon has been seen hunting south of the valley. We don't want to lose anyone. The warden will guide you if the dragon moves into your area. It's policy. You know."

"But—"

But it would be impossible to secretly sample a communion mound if a warden accompanied them. Still, there was no point in getting involved in a useless argument they could not win. It would only draw suspicion. So Skye put her hand on Buyu's arm. "Don't worry about it," she said softly. "We've all had babysitters before." They would simply have to find a way around the warden.

Buyu gave her a strange look, as if he knew there was some hidden plan behind her words, but couldn't fathom what it might be. Skye only wished she knew.

"Skye's right," Devi said. "What's another babysitter? We're only raw ados after all."

Matilé smiled, but it was a cold expression. Devi's sarcasm had obviously annoyed her. "Have fun, then. And I promise, you'll hardly see the warden—unless something goes wrong." She said this last in a harsher tone, so that Skye felt sure she suspected them of something unsavory.

What did Sensei Matilé remember of being an ado? If she were like most real people she would remember it badly, as if being an ado was all about raw passions and bad judgment. The term *dumb ado* wasn't so much an insult as a description of expected behavior. And if ados really did act stupid from time to time, that proved the rule, didn't it?

⁓

They set out on foot along the road. One tour group had gone south, straight into the forest. To look for the acid dragon, perhaps? The rest had flown down to the coastal settlements. So the four of them were alone—except for the warden, of course.

The little green-glass humanoid spy followed them as they left the terminal building. Skye saw it for only a few seconds before it disappeared among the trees, its surface transforming into a collage of green-brown shadows that let it blend into the vegetation. Ord's tentacle *tap-tapped* at her throat. "Skye is angry," it whispered. "Why?"

"I'm okay."

No one else said anything.

They hiked half a kilometer, and still no one talked.

Skye stroked Ord's long tentacle, thinking, *What a miserable bunch we are.* Zia was plodding along, gazing at her feet, her brow wrinkled with worry. Devi glared at nothing, still quietly furious. Buyu trudged in silence, a distraught expression on his face.

Buyu had a right to worry. He was risking more than anyone else by being here. If they were caught violating rules, it was Buyu who would be held responsible. He might be suspended forever from the explorer corps.

As Skye thought about this, she almost turned back . . . until she remembered, *this isn't about me.* They were here to find a cure for Compassion, not for her sake, but for the other children from her great ship, lost somewhere in the void in lifeboats of their own.

If it was only about me, Skye thought, I would check into the monkey house right now.

Well. If they had to be here, if it was the only thing to do, then they might as well make the most of it. Right?

She grinned mischievously. In the middle of the roadway she stopped to draw in a deep breath of forest air, filling herself with the scents of humus, sunlight, and unseen flowers. Then she let it all out again in a long, drawn-out whoop that echoed off the valley walls, "*Yee-oww!*"

Ord startled, slipping halfway down her back. Buyu jumped so hard he almost fell down. Devi spun around as if the acid dragon were charging him from behind. Zia looked like she'd been frozen. One glance at their shocked faces and Skye started laughing so hard her belly hurt. "You . . . all," she stammered, gasping for air, "are the most . . . depressing lot of ados I have ever run with. Look at this beautiful world! This is the first time we've ever been on any world . . . except for Buyu of course . . . but you all haven't even looked at it yet! Open your eyes. Open your lungs! Stop moping, because if you think that warden's going to slow us down, you don't know me at all."

"It occurs to me," Devi said, "that I really don't know you at all."

She winked at him, as Ord climbed back up on her shoulder, and tapped at her neck. "Something to look forward to, then."

"This is serious, Skye."

"Sooth. But we haven't been defeated yet . . . unless you all have changed your minds?"

That drew a chorus of denials.

"Skye's right," Zia said. "We're giving up too easily. There's got to be a way to lose our warden."

Buyu shook his head. "I don't know how."

"Could we split up?" Skye asked.

"I'd be suspended for it," Buyu said. "And the warden would only summon another."

Zia gazed anxiously into the forest on the southern side of the road, where the warden had disappeared. "Should we be talking about this?"

"It's probably okay," Devi said. "The wardens usually run themselves, though it is possible that some bored handler in the city could be monitoring what it sees and hears."

"We should be careful," Buyu said. "Did you see Sensei Matilé? She knew something was up."

Skye hit Buyu with a wicked smile. "Buyu, just for a minute, pretend you were Sensei Matilé, and you saw two nervous-looking ado boys with two nervous-looking ado girls, heading off for a day alone in the wilderness, and—my my!—how upset they are at having a warden along *watching* them. If you were as real as Sensei Matilé, what would *you* think?"

There was silence for several seconds, and then Devi and Zia erupted in laughter, while Buyu flushed red up to his ears. It took him a few minutes before he could manage any response at all, and even then it was only to point out, "That still doesn't solve our problem."

"I'm thinking about it," Skye said. "Give me time."

After that, they talked and laughed on the long hike out of the valley. When they reached the crest of the ridge, they paused for a few minutes to look back at the huge black terminal building, and the massive gray pillar of the elevator column rising up into the sky like a giant shaft driven through the world's heart. Skye squinted, but she could not make out the bulge of Silk 300 kilometers overhead.

"So which way from here?" Zia asked, gesturing with a juice bottle that she had scavenged from Buyu's pack. The road ended at the ridge top. It had been built by Silk's original people a long time ago, and it never had been put to formal use. Modern Silkens traveled either by air or on foot, to cause the least disturbance to the biosphere.

"The acid dragon is supposed to be south," Buyu said. "So let's head the other way, up into the mountains. There's a stream just over this ridge. We can follow it up. There are pools and waterfalls all the way. Lots of opportunity there."

Skye smiled at his choice of words. No one had dared to say "communion mound" since last night.

A stir of camouflaged motion caught her eye. She stared at the brush, and after several seconds she was able to pick out the concealed shape of the warden. So their babysitter remained close by. "Maybe if we go south," she growled, "we could get the acid dragon to eat our friend."

Buyu followed her gaze. "You don't want that. If the acid dragon got the warden, it's sure we'd be its next bite. Those things are bad news . . . and I haven't updated my personal file in a long time."

Skye frowned at this reminder. A personal file was a formal record of the precise physical structure of a human being, exact down to the individual links between brain cells, where memory was recorded. If something happened to them here in the Well, they could each be rebuilt by a fleet of resurrection Makers working from the pattern in their personal file ... but like Buyu, Skye hadn't updated hers in ages. The person recorded in her file was a naive thirteen year old. *How could I have overlooked something so obvious?*

"I did mine last night," Zia admitted guiltily.

Skye laughed. "At least one of us has some brains."

Devi was gazing up into the mountains. "You're pretty smart yourself, Skye."

She glanced up the slope. These mountains guarded the coast of the southern continent. They were heavily eroded, with steep valleys gouged between knife-edge ridges. Rain forest grew all the way to the summit, where fluffy white clouds were beginning to gather. She looked back at Devi. He was watching her with a half-smile on his face and a thoughtful look in his eyes that she could not resist. Hands on her hips, she demanded to know, "What are you thinking?"

His smile widened. "Let's just do what Buyu says. Follow the stream. See what we can find."

They saw their first communion mound on the way down to the stream. It sprouted from the ground at the base of a fallen tree. It didn't look like much, just a knob of upthrust soil, thigh-high and maybe two meters across. Its surface resembled matted mud with a green algae sheen. Skye and Zia rushed toward it, but Buyu held out his hands, blocking the way. "We're not supposed to get within five meters," he said softly. The warden was a shimmer of motion in the shrubbery. "There are lots of mounds," he added, almost in a whisper.

Skye nodded and moved back half a step. "What are communion mounds?" she asked. "What do you know about them?"

He shrugged. "Nobody knows much. They're some kind of Chenzeme biotech, but their original purpose has probably been changed by the Well governors. They keep track of information, especially if it has to do with humans. The strangest thing about them is that they've only existed for a few hundred years, only since the original builders of Silk died . . . of . . ." His voice trailed off in guilty silence.

"Of plague," Skye finished for him, as she stroked one of Ord's tentacles. "It wasn't a Chenzeme plague, though. The people of Old Silk didn't understand the Well's microscopic governors. They released a destructive Maker—and the governors fought back."

"Sooth."

She smiled at him. "Buyu, don't look so worried. Please. You're scaring me."

"It's just that . . . anything could be in the mounds. Good things, bad things. It's why they're off-limits."

"Listen," Devi interrupted. "You can hear the stream."

They followed the noise down to the bottom of a shallow gulch, where the stream splashed and chattered through a channel of polished rock and smooth boulders. The water was a beautiful, dilute emerald green, and thicker than normal water should be. Zia had been studying planetary biology for several months. She dipped her hands into it and explained, "It's full of long, complex molecules that carry information in chemical form. Think of it as a library belonging to the Well's governors. You can drink it"— she lifted a handful of the green water to her lips to prove it was so— "and it won't harm you, though some say it will record everything about you."

"So who needs a personal file?" Skye joked.

"Anybody who wants to find their file again," Zia said, without a hint of her usual good humor.

Trees growing on the gully walls leaned over the stream, casting cool shadows that pressed against the water, smoothing its surface so that the pebbles and the tiny aquatic creatures that foraged on the bottom could be easily seen. Where the stream flowed into sunlight, the water glittered with bright, dancing reflections.

The first waterfall they came to boiled noisily over a broad, curved ledge only a meter high. A quiet pool fanned out from the base of the little fall; bubbles skated over its calm surface. The pool looked to be maybe two and a half meters deep. Skye could see through the green water, all the way to the boulder-strewn bottom.

Devi and Buyu were walking ahead, discussing biology and predators and annoying little wardens as they looked for a dry path around the side of the waterfall. Skye touched Zia's elbow. "Hey, ado. Let's swim."

Zia looked at her, wide-eyed. "You're kidding."

"Be safe, Skye," Ord said. "Check water first." It lowered itself from her shoulder to the sun-warmed rocks. Then it scuttled to the edge of the water, dipping its tentacles into the pool.

Skye and Zia crouched beside it. "Clean?" Skye asked.

"There are many life forms, but they are not immediately hazardous—"

"Immediately?" Zia asked nervously.

"Zia Adovna," Skye whispered. "You jump like a maniac off the elevator column. You can't be afraid to go for a little swim."

Zia stared at the water. "I'm not afraid."

Devi and Buyu had reached the top of the waterfall. Buyu had gone on ahead, but Devi was looking back at them curiously. Skye put on her sweetest smile. "Zia, this is your last warning. I'm going to dive on three. One, two—"

Zia sprang first, diving into the quiet water, sending a green fountain bubbling into the morning air. Skye followed a second later, knifing beneath the surface, feeling the icy shock of the water against her face. Then she burst to the surface in the middle of the pool with a whoop that echoed off the gully walls.

Zia was already stroking for the little waterfall. Skye raced after her. They glided under the falling water, letting the cold stream pound against their backs. Kheth glinted through the trees, turning the falling drops diamond bright. She could see Ord following after them, a shimmering golden shape just beneath the surface, its tentacles whipping behind it like a long, sinuous tail.

"Skye!" Devi yelled from somewhere overhead, his voice almost lost within the noise of rushing water. "Get serious. You're just wasting time!"

"Be an ado, ado," she yelled back. "And stop worrying so much. I am not going to die."

She crouched on a shelf of submerged rock, just under the fall. How strange—the way the water rippled, it looked as if the boulders on the bottom were moving. Skye watched the effect for several seconds, until she realized it wasn't an illusion. Several large, submerged boulders *were* moving. They were slowly crawling away from the waterfall. "Zia . . . ?"

"I see it, ado. Maybe we should rejoin the boys?"

Skye stood up, craning to get a better view of the bottom. The boulder beneath her feet was slick and soft with a layer of brown algae. "But what is it?"

"I don't know. I've only studied the planet from a microbiologist's point of view. If it's big enough to see with the unaided eye, I don't know anything about it."

Skye felt a lurch under her feet. She struggled to keep her balance on the slick, algae-covered boulder. Or was it a boulder?

Zia had felt the movement too. "What say we get out of here?"

"Swimming?" Skye asked uncertainly.

Zia looked over her shoulder, where a line of exposed rock broke the smooth curtain of the waterfall. "I'm climbing."

The boulder under Skye's feet shifted again. Then something soft and strong caught her ankle. It felt like a huge, powerful hand. Panic kicked in. With a yelp, she brought her other foot down hard against the thing that held her. Apparently it didn't like that at all, because it let go. In fact, it shoved her hard. She lost her balance and plunged into the pool. With her eyes open, she spun around, and through the clear green water she watched the boulder glide away across the bottom.

She kicked hard, and shot to the surface, spluttering. Then she swam furiously for the waterfall. Zia was already clambering over the top. Skye got a hand on a slippery outcropping of rock just above the level of the pool. (This time, she made sure it was rock.) She climbed onto it, while the waterfall splashed around her. Then she looked back.

One of the "boulders" had glided into the shallow water on the far side of the pool. As she watched, it broke the surface. It did not look so much like a rock anymore. It glistened with a warm, brown, velvety texture—and it was big. Perhaps a meter high and a meter across. As it emerged from the water its surface split open, revealing folds of bright pink tissue . . . and a second later it let loose a horrible screech that sent a hundred hidden flyers leaping from the trees into the air. Skye scrambled over the little waterfall in a panic, hardly conscious of the treacherous nature of the slippery rock, or what would happen if she fell.

She rolled out over the top, into a three inch deep flow of water that swept across a shelf of grey rock. Devi and Buyu were laughing themselves silly, while Zia was sitting on the rocky bank, looking embarrassed and beaten. Down in the pond, three other boulders had poked their mouths above the surface, to raise their own ear-splitting cries of indignation. "What is that?" Skye snapped.

Devi only laughed harder. Buyu tried to catch his breath long enough to say. "Hungry rocks. They eat small water life. They may actually farm some of the more common species, but they definitely don't like anything else hunting in their home pond."

"It grabbed my foot!" Skye told him. "It tried to pull me under."

"It can't pull, Skye," Buyu said. "It doesn't have the necessary joints or muscles—"

"Like you know!" She climbed to her feet. "I felt it."

"Hey," Devi said. "Buyu's just telling you the way it is. The hungry rock probably thought your foot was its usual prey. It's about at the upper size limit, wouldn't you say, Buyu? If the rock didn't realize your foot was attached to a much larger body—"

Skye's eyes went wide in shock. "Ord!" she yelled. "Where did Ord go?"

She scrambled back to the edge of the waterfall along with Zia and Devi. They peered over the edge. Ord was nowhere to be seen.

Skye's hands closed into helpless fists. "Oh no," she whispered. "Ord would be prey-size, wouldn't it?"

"*Gutter dogs*," Devi muttered. "We're helpless without Ord."

Just then a stream of bubbles shot from the top of one of the hungry rocks that had remained underwater. A foul odor—worse than a gutter doggie's dump tunnel—burst onto the air. Then through the green water, Skye saw the rock's mouth open. A huge golden bubble erupted from it like a silent burp. It rose to the surface where it burst open, releasing a horrible scent-bomb of bad odor. Zia shrieked. Devi groaned. Skye felt her stomach churning . . . but there was Ord! It swam calmly toward the waterfall, propelled by the lash of its long tentacles.

"Ord!" Skye shouted. She climbed back down the waterfall, holding out a hand to the little robot. It swung its tentacle forward and caught her wrist. She hefted it up, laughing. "You scared me, you dumb little thing."

"Good Skye," it whispered. "Too cold for swimming, yes Skye?"

She laughed in giddy relief as she swung Ord up to the top of the fall. "You know, you may be right."

Chapter 10

Skye's mood cooled after that. She started thinking more and more about how they might get rid of the warden without getting Buyu in trouble, but the only idea that seemed at all promising was her original notion of using the warden as bait for the acid dragon. She was about to suggest it again, when Devi suddenly stopped. He'd been out in front. Now he dropped into a crouch behind a waist-high boulder, peering over the top at something Skye could not see, while waving at the rest of them to *keep down*. He took one more look, then he crept back to meet them. "There's a litter of viperlion pups in the next pool," he whispered.

Viperlions?

Skye frowned. "Isn't that some kind of a—"

"A predator," Zia whispered. "I've heard of them."

Devi nodded. He kept his voice low as he added, "It's pretty common to find the pups along stream banks. They can slip into the water to avoid danger. They're able to stay under for several minutes—assuming there aren't any hungry rocks in the pool." He looked at Skye with a self-satisfied smile. "They're more common at higher elevations. I thought we might have to hike a long way to find some."

"I'm not hearing this," Buyu muttered. He backed several steps away. Then he gazed across the stream, as if he was alone in the wilderness and they were not plotting treason behind his back.

Skye looked at Devi. His cheeks were a rosy brown, flush with the equatorial heat. His eyes seemed to be asking her, *Are you in?*

She thought she could guess his plan. Quickly she scanned the thickets, but she saw no sign of the warden. "Viperlions are pretty aggressive?" she whispered.

Zia had just caught on too. She looked suddenly frantic. Her head whipped around as she searched for the warden. "You two are crazy."

"What else are we going to do?" Devi whispered.

"I don't know."

"Will the parent be close by?" Skye asked.

"I hope so."

Zia said, "How are we going to make sure it gets the warden and not us?"

Devi's smile was apologetic. "I don't know. Any ideas?"

Skye hefted Ord onto her shoulder. "Let you know in a minute. First I'm going to take a look." She glanced at Buyu, but he was still staring off into the bushes, pretending he didn't know what was going on.

They had come to a place where the stream ran fast and narrow. Skye waded into the water until it reached her waist. Then she made her way upstream, holding onto plants that grew along the bank to keep her balance. The streambed wound to the left, around a polished gray rock twice her height. She edged past it, to find a broad, shallow pool on the other side, formed behind a natural dam of melon-sized rocks. Seven little creatures, each no bigger than a dokey, chased and wrestled one another on the margin of the pool, where the water was only a few inches deep. Each one moved on six ribbon-like legs—legs that were much wider from front to back than from side to side—tapering to small, clawed feet, so that it looked as if each viperlion was walking on three pairs of oversized tweezers.

Most of the animal life of Earth was built on a lateral plan—in a line—so that mouth/brain/eyes were at one end, digestive and reproductive organs were in the middle, and waste was eliminated at the other end. In contrast, much of the animal life of Deception Well was built on a radial plan—in a circle—around central digestive organs, like a sea star from Earth, except the basic radial layout had undergone a lot of change. Evolution had led it to imitate the lateral plan, so that the viperlions had head and tail at opposite ends of a long, sinuous body. In fact they had two heads each, and two . . . *maws.* That was the proper word, Skye recalled. Not mouths, because viperlions did not swallow food through their long necks. Their "necks" were really just modified legs from the ancient circle of legs that was the basic plan for life on this planet. Each head had two eyes, and one set of grasping and tearing "jaws," though the jaws might as well be called toothy pincers.

As Skye watched, one of the pups jumped thirty centimeters in the air. One of its heads darted out, its maw dropped open, and it snapped up a passing insect. It crunched hard. Then its snake-like neck swung under its belly, tucking the insect into its central stomach before its litter-mates could grab a share. Its tail waved proudly, looking like a thick noodle with a pom-pom on the end. Another viperlion pup leaped on its back. The four-heads dueled, before both pups went rolling through the water.

Skye grinned. These pups were the cutest things she had seen since dokeys.

A twitch of motion drew her gaze to the thickets beyond the stream's gravel bank. She expected to see the warden there, watching, making sure all the rules were being followed, but if it was there, it was too well-camouflaged for her to see it.

Ord shifted restlessly. Skye looked around to find that Devi had slipped up beside her. He was submerged to his neck, so she sank down beside him. "Have you seen the warden?" she whispered.

"No."

"It might be over there"—she nodded toward the thickets across the stream—"but I'm not—"

She left her whispered sentence unfinished as a blue-winged bat dropped out of the sky. Or maybe it wasn't a bat. It had wings that were bat-like—made of thin skin stretched between long bones—but its eyes were in its belly, and there were pincer-limbs attached to the front and back of its disc-like body, each midway between the glistening wings. It fell toward a pup that had wandered alone to one end of the gravel bank. It held its blue wings high as it reached with its pincer-limbs to grab the baby.

But just as it was about to strike, a snake-like head with glittering black eyes reared up from the thickets where Skye had thought the warden might be hidden. The head looked like a quarter-sized model of a transit car. The neck that carried it was thicker than the posts that held up the footbridge at Vibrant Harmony. As the head darted out over the gravel bank—looking like the head of a giant, floating snake, unaffected by gravity—its jaw gaped open, exposing a bright red maw more than large enough to crunch Skye's skull. It snapped up the blue flyer, crushing it instantly and smearing its wings into odd angles.

The parent viperlion.

Skye eased back into the shadow of the rock while Ord patted her cheeks. "Go home now, Skye?" it whispered.

As the viperlion's head withdrew into the bushes with its prey, a second head emerged, sweeping protectively over the pups with the same dreamy floating motion.

Skye felt a tap on her shoulder. She turned to find Devi crooking a finger at her. He wanted her to slide back down the stream and behind the rocks. She shook her head. Instead, she started angling across the current, making for the far bank. "*Skye!*" Devi hissed.

She turned around and laid a finger over her mouth in a plea for silence. Then she held her palm up, urging him to *stay*. Quickly, she crossed the stream and climbed the far bank. She could see Buyu and Zia, watching her with puzzled faces. Devi was still standing in the stream, the water up to his waist, looking undecided. She reached up to touch Ord's smooth side. "Hold on tight," she warned, in a barely audible whisper.

"No good, Skye," Ord whispered back. "Time to go home now, yes? Yes, it is. Go home. Go home now, good Skye."

Skye patted it again. Then she ducked into the bushes and began creeping up the stream bank. A splash warned her that someone was following. *Zeme dust!* She wanted to yell at them to stay back, but when she turned to look, she found that everyone remained exactly where she had left them. Well, good.

She crept through the bushes, trying to reach a point above the stream exactly opposite the half-hidden viperlion.

Suddenly, the warden appeared in front of her only half a meter away, blocking her path. It had been so well hidden it seemed to materialize out of nowhere. At first its face was blank, with only a suggestion of eyes, nose, and mouth. Then its features shifted and deepened. She found herself looking at a petite copy of Buyu's face. "Skye," he growled, "don't make me tell you again. Get back here now, or your right to visit the planet will be suspended for five years. You know it's illegal to approach a predator like the viperlion."

Skye grinned. She'd come up the stream bank hoping to make the warden nervous so it would show itself, but this was more than perfect. Buyu had used his authority as a guide to tap into the warden. He couldn't override its behavior, but his terse warning would keep him looking honest and responsible—and hopefully keep him out of trouble—without interfering with her plans at all.

Buyu, you are slick!

"Get back now," the warden commanded, in stern imitation of Buyu's voice.

"Sure!" Skye said, as loudly as she could manage. She stood up abruptly, rattling bushes. "I just wanted to get a closer look at those pups!"

Several things happened at once:

The adult viperlion's two heads rose together above the thickets, both of them staring across the stream, straight at Skye.

A soft grunting arose from the brush and the pups responded, disappearing immediately among the swaying plants.

The warden slipped down to the water, its path marked by rustling bushes.

And Ord clung a little more tightly to Skye's neck. "Bad, bad, bad," it whispered. "See it? No good. Go home, Skye. Be silent. Be safe. Please good Skye?"

The viperlion glided out of the thicket. There was no other way Skye could think to describe it. Its snake-like heads floated out first, then its arched body followed, narrow and sinuous and mottled green, so that it might easily slip between trees or slide under logs and still match the background color of the forest. Its six ribbon legs balanced on tiny feet that hardly seemed to touch the ground. Its tail followed behind: a two meter whip with a tassel at the end.

Skye started backing away up the steep slope.

From the corner of her eye, she saw Devi and Zia floundering across the stream. Buyu remained on the far bank. The tall gray rocks still kept them all hidden from the viperlion's gaze.

Buyu was using his suit radio to talk to someone. Skye was startled, and for a moment she was overcome with doubt. Maybe Buyu wasn't the one in control of the warden? Maybe city authority had only used his voice, thinking she would be more likely to listen? How dangerous were viperlions, anyway?

Zia and Devi reached the stream bank. They scrambled toward Skye, crushing bushes, snapping branches, sending pebbles rolling toward the water. The noise angered the staring viperlion. Both its maws opened, flashing a red warning. Then it charged.

Ord shrieked. It was the loudest sound Skye had ever heard the robot make, but she didn't need any encouragement to run. She turned and scrambled up the gully wall, pulling on stems and tree trunks to haul herself higher.

The viperlion required only two bounds to cross the natural rock dam that had created the pool. Water fountained beneath its tiny feet, and then it reached the gravel bank. It was met by the warden, which appeared as if from nowhere. The startled viperlion skidded to a stop. Skye hesitated too, turning to watch the confrontation.

The warden had given up its camouflage colors. Instead of blending in with the foliage, its color had changed to bright red, and as she watched its body stretched into an absurdly tall, absurdly thin figure, like a paper cut-out.

The viperlion wasn't fooled, though—or else it just didn't care how big its prey appeared to be. It dropped into a crouch, and its two heads darted forward, attacking the warden from opposite sides. The maws snapped. One closed on the warden's shoulder. The other grabbed it by the hip. When the heads jerked back, the warden flew apart in a great splash of red gelatinous goo. The remains of the warden trailed from the maws as they swung back, tucking their prizes into the viperlion's underbelly stomach.

"Run!" Devi shouted. "Skye! Get over the ridge and out of sight!"

Skye was just about to take his advice when the branch she'd been holding snapped. She lost her footing on the steep slope and went down, sliding on her rear through the broken bushes. The viperlion heard the noise, and gave up on retrieving the scattered remains of the warden. It called out in a hooting growl. Then it charged again, rushing up the slope on its six ribbon legs, moving with a terrifying, mechanical smoothness.

Skye grabbed at the brush to stop her slide. She got her feet back under her. Giving up on climbing out of the gully, she turned, scrambling upstream, shattering bushes in her path. Behind her, Devi was whooping, trying to distract the viperlion . . . but it had already chosen its prey.

She burst out of the bushes, only to find herself facing a wall of rough, gray stone. The stream was now several meters below her, dropping down a series of steep rapids. It was too wide to jump, and too shallow to hide in. She would have to climb the wall.

She leaped, grabbing for a knob of rock half a meter above her head. She got her hand on it, but the knob snapped off. She tumbled to the ground, landing on her back, hard. The air was knocked out of her lungs. She lay there a second, staring at the bright blue sky and listening to the crackle of the viperlion's approach. "Up, Skye, up," Ord pleaded, patting her neck. "Go home now. Be safe."

A gust of cold air flowed over her cheek. She turned her head and saw a dark hole, barely half a meter wide and only twenty centimeters high, in the bottom of the gray stone wall. It was half-hidden behind shrubs, with moss growing around the entrance and some kind of white scat on the ground in front of it. Another gust of cold air flowed out of the hole . . . which meant it had another entrance somewhere!

She flopped over just as the viperlion bounded out of the thicket. It hesitated, confused, perhaps, by her position on the ground, for after all, it had been expecting a tall, slender lunch. Skye used the moment to scramble on her elbows, wriggling headfirst into the narrow opening, willing it to be deep enough to shelter her whole body. As she jammed her shoulders in, dirt scraped off the walls. Roots slapped her face. The viperlion huffed and growled. It sounded as if it were right behind her.

She scrambled faster. She got her shoulders in, her waist, her hips and then her legs. She still had not come to the end of the dark tunnel; a frigid breeze whispered past her face, coaxing her onward.

She surged forward. She was going to make it! The viperlion was way too big to follow her into this little hole.

Then a horrible pressure closed over her right foot. The viperlion had bit her with its maw! The scales of her skin suit responded instantly, locking into place around her leg, freezing into a diamond-hard protective armor that prevented her foot from being crushed. The warden's soft biogel body had been shredded by the viperlion. Her suit was tougher than that, but it could not make the viperlion let go. The creature hauled back on her foot, trying to drag her out of the burrow. Skye fought it. She dug her gloved fingers into the sparse soil. She clung to knobs of rock, and wedged her elbows against the tunnel walls, but it was a losing battle. Slowly, slowly, the viperlion was dragging her out.

She kicked its snout with her other foot. She screamed at it: "Let go of me you mindless biomachine! I am not your babies' lunch!"

As if in reply, it yanked her back another ten centimeters.

Her arms trembled with exhaustion. Ord was whispering something in her ear, but she couldn't understand it. "What? What?"

How long could her skin suit protect her, if the viperlion got her outside?

Ord disappeared. Skye felt it clambering along her back, slipping through the narrow space beneath the tunnel roof. Did Ord think it could force the viperlion to let her go? Ord was made of biogel! The viperlion could shred it with a single bite. "Ord! Get back here!"

Then suddenly, the same horrible odor Skye had smelled at the hungry rock pond filled the tunnel in an invisible, noxious cloud. She dropped her nose to her arm with a retching yell of disgust. Her eyes watered, and she was instantly nauseous.

The viperlion let go.

It took Skye a moment to realize it, but the pressure on her foot was gone. Were the viperlion's eyes stinging as badly as her own?

She charged forward again on elbows and knees, dirt raining down on her neck, until at last she was sure she'd gone far enough that even with its long neck, the viperlion couldn't reach her.

But did that mean it would be hunting for Devi and Zia and Buyu now?

At once, Skye started to turn around—only to realize she had crawled beyond the tunnel, into a lightless cavern, where the harsh sound of her breathing echoed off unseen walls. When she tried to turn back, she bumped into rock. She felt for the passage, but it wasn't where she expected to find it. She peered into the darkness, searching for some distant glimmer of daylight, but there was nothing. The tunnel must have turned without her realizing it, cutting off any light.

"Ord?" Her voice sounded faint in the darkness. She raised her head cautiously, but the roof was high enough that she didn't bump into it. "Ord?" she repeated.

She heard a clattering of limbs against stone. "*Ord?*" Her voice slid into unstable high notes.

"Yes good Skye. Quiet and safe now. Yes. But you should go home."

She heard the viperlion huffing and snorting somewhere nearby. She tried to follow the sound, but in the lightless cave it seemed to come from everywhere at once. So at least the viperlion wasn't hunting the others. Not yet. If they were smart, they would use this time to get far away—but they wouldn't run away unless they knew she was okay . . . would they?

"Ord, can you reach Buyu's suit radio?"

Several seconds passed, then, "No, Skye."

"Maybe if you crawl out to the edge of the tunnel? Can you find your way out?"

"Yes Skye."

"Tell them to get away. There's got to be another way out of this cave. I'll look for it, and meet them when I get out. And Ord—"

"Yes Skye?"

"Don't get eaten, okay?"

"Okay, Skye."

She listened to Ord scuttle away. Then she stood up, cautiously feeling for a roof, but there was nothing. It occurred to her to talk to her suit DI. "Is there a function for light?" she asked.

The suit answered in its soft, feminine voice. "Yes. The surface scales are capable of luminescence in any designated pattern."

Well, *slick*.

"Light them all," Skye commanded.

The skin suit began to glow. At first the illumination was a soft blue, but it grew gradually brighter, casting blue light just the color of her suit across the high walls and ceiling of a long cavern. The chamber was at least three times her height. The light of her skin suit did not reach to the far end. Trailing ropes hung from the ceiling. It took her a moment to realize they were the roots of plants growing on the slope above the cave. Water dripped from them, and from the cave roof, which was encrusted with a dull layer of bubbly, light-colored stone that looked blue in the blue light of her suit.

She could still hear the snuffling of the viperlion, which discouraged the idea of trying to get out the same way she had gotten
in. She could wait for it to leave, but that might take all day. If
she didn't get back to the elevator on time, rescuers would come
after her, and she would never get a chance to explore the mounds.
Rescuers might be coming already, responding to the loss of the
warden. Were the devices monitored that closely? She didn't know,
but clearly time was limited. She needed to get out of this cave and
find a mound before the opportunity was lost forever.

"Ord?"

"Coming, Skye." Its voice sounded distant. "Buyu and Zia and
Devi report they are safe." Its limbs rattled on rock as it scuttled
into sight. She realized she was looking at the passage. It was such
a tiny hole! Had she really come in through that?

Ord crouched, assuming a look of concentration. Then Devi's
voice emerged from its mouth. "Skye, it sounds like you're in a lava
tube. Be careful, because there could be pits in the floor, or loose
rock on the ceiling. Let Ord go first. We'll move upslope, and try
to find the other entrance . . . but hey ado, at least you got rid of
the warden."

Skye grinned. Well, yeah. That had been the whole point, hadn't
it? "Come on, Ord," she said. "Let's find another way out of here."

Chapter 11

The floor of the cave was treacherous, with massive slabs of steeply slanting rock, and piles of rubble where parts of the ceiling had collapsed. Yet, taken as a whole, the cave was remarkably orderly. It ran upslope in roughly a straight line, and while the walls were made of jagged lava, the passage itself was still regular enough that it might have been drilled out of the original rock.

Ord scrambled ahead, looking for the best path. Skye hurried to keep up, thankful for the cold breeze in her face that assured her there *was* another way out. At one point they came to a Y-shaped junction, where the cave branched in two directions. Ord hesitated, its tentacles spread as it tested the air. Then it scurried down the left side.

"What exactly is a lava tube?" Skye asked.

Ord replied, "City library does not respond."

"Oh. The radio signal can't get out of this cave." Never before had Ord failed to answer such a simple factual question. It gave her a strangely vulnerable feeling.

They walked on for another fifteen minutes. Finally, Skye was able to make out a gray glimmer in the distance. The light brightened as they approached. It fell from overhead, onto a cone-shaped pile of tumbled rocks, twice as tall as her own considerable height. The light had an odd, gray-green quality. She approached the site with a growing sense of gloom.

Clearly, the cave roof had fallen in, creating the pile of rubble and opening up a skylight to the outside world. The trouble was, the cave roof was at least ten meters overhead. Climbing the pile of rubble would get her halfway there, but she would still be a long way from getting out.

Ord said, "A lava tube is a channel formed by fast-moving lava when the surface of the flow cools and hardens. This crust insulates the superhot lava beneath, which continues to flow, sometimes for days. When the eruption stops, the lava drains out of the channel, leaving behind a long, tubular cave."

Skye smiled. "Are you in contact with city library again, Ord?"

"Yes Skye."

The cave continued on past the skylight. No telling how far. She squinted into the darkness, wondering if it was worth pushing on. "What do you think, Ord? Is there another entrance farther up?"

"Good to check," Ord said, and scrambled away.

While it was gone, Skye climbed the rock pile, pausing every few steps to listen for Devi or Zia calling. She heard nothing. She reached the top of the mound and balanced there, gazing up at a canopy of leaves in a hundred shades of green. A flock of small red flyers fluttered and darted through the branches. The day seemed very dim. No sunlight glinted between the leaves, and after a minute she realized that a heavy layer of clouds had gathered across the sky.

Ord reappeared. "No good, Skye. Bad air."

"Okay, Ord. Then we get out this way."

It occurred to her she could toss Ord out. It could sample any mounds in the neighborhood. The job would be done. Then she could just wait here until rescue arrived.

Of course then Buyu would be in deep, deep trouble for losing her. Maybe he already was, but she would hope for the best. She would hope city authority hadn't yet noticed that anything was wrong.

She drew in a deep breath, then yelled as loudly as she could, "*Zia!*" Her voice echoed off the cave wall and off the trees, and the red flyers scattered. "Zia! Devi! Buyu!" Again the echoes rolled away.

This time though, someone answered, sounding not too far off. "Skye?"

"Devi! Down here! Watch out for a big hole in the ground!"

"Keep talking, Skye! I'm following your voice."

"Here. I'm over here, but I can't get out. Are you all right? Where's Zia?"

"Right here," Zia said, sticking her head over the rim of the hole. She had dirt and bits of leaves stuck in her wiry hair, but her usual good humor had returned. She grinned at Skye's predicament. "You look like some kind of goddess on her altar . . . only the ground fell out from under you." She snickered.

"Ha ha. How am I going to get out of here?"

Devi's head appeared beside Zia. He had lost the tie for his ponytail; his red and blond hair fell forward over his face as he looked down. He shoved one side of it behind an ear. "Are you all right?"

"Sooth. How am I going to get out of here?"

Buyu said, "I've got a rope."

She turned to see him standing at a low point on the rim of the skylight. He had dropped his pack at his feet. Now he uncoiled a strand of orange rope. As he lowered it into the cave, loops sprouted every half meter along its length. Skye scrambled down the pile of rocks, but Ord reached the rope first. "Check for safety, Skye." It scrambled up the line, testing each loop as it formed.

"We're set," Buyu called down. "Climb up when you're ready."

"Sooth. I'm coming now."

Each loop hardened as she touched it, making a perfect step. It was an easy climb. When she reached the point where the rope lay against the rim of the skylight, each loop arched up a little, so she could get her fingers all the way around it. In a few more steps, she rolled out onto a padding of fallen leaves, and laughed. "What an adventure! Buyu, I couldn't believe it when you took control of that warden. It was amazing!"

"The whole thing was stupid," Buyu snapped. He held up his finger and thumb, only a centimeter apart. "You came this close to being lunch for that viperlion. When was the last time you updated your personal record?"

She couldn't remember. What did it matter? She'd gotten away. Though Buyu was right—it had been close. "It bit my foot," she said, sitting up. "The skin suit hardened."

"The skin suit wouldn't have saved you if it had gotten its maw on your skull. Did it ever occur to you to put your hood up? Coming down here was a big mistake. Only dumb ados would come up with a plan like this. No wonder they didn't want me on an exploration team!"

She stared at him in shock. She had never seen Buyu angry before. He was certainly showing an unwelcome range of emotions lately. She looked to Zia and Devi for help. Devi only looked confused. Zia nodded. "Take it easy, Buyu. It may not have been the most elegant plan, but it worked."

"That's right," Skye said. "Don't forget why we're down here."

"You should be in the monkey house," Buyu countered.

Her temper snapped. "*Gutter dogs!* Buyu, the mounds were your idea, and it was a good idea. It's still a good idea, so let's do it while we have the chance. Okay?"

He looked like he wanted to argue, but there was no good argument to make. He nodded. "All right. I saw a mound about twenty meters down the ridge."

They had just set out when a pattering sound swept across the canopy. Skye looked up, curious and a little concerned. "What—?" Droplets of water splashed on her face and she ducked her head, spluttering.

"Rain," Buyu said.

Devi held out his hands to feel the fat, cold drops falling off the trees. On his face was a look of wonder. "*Rain*. This is so wild! Water, just falling out of the sky."

Skye wiped the water off her face, but more kept falling from the leaves . . . or from the clouds, that was it. Rain. She had seen rain in virtual reality stories, but she had never felt it before. It was cold, and she wasn't sure she liked it.

They found the mound a minute later. It was small, only about half a meter across and knee-high. It looked like it was made of matted soil, or half-rotted mulch. Nothing grew on its surface. Mounds were nanotech factories, and they were said to be hot. She laid her gloved hand against it. The glove translated the feel of anything she touched; raw heat soaked into her palm. The mound had to be at least fifteen degrees above human body temperature. A light mist steamed off its surface as the rain struck.

Mounds were Chenzeme devices modified by the Well governors. They were supposed to collect data on human beings . . . and the plagues that could affect them? Skye hoped so. "Okay Ord," she said, stepping back at last. "It's up to you now. Can you find evidence of the Compassion plague? And can you find a cure?" Among all the long, green, data-bearing molecules that crawled through the Well's biosphere and colored its water, there had to be some smart molecular machine that could defeat the Chenzeme nanotech weapon she carried in her cells.

"City library agrees it is possible," Ord said. "Skye is very smart to know this. Good Skye."

"Now, Ord."

"Yes."

She looked at Devi. He smiled encouragement. Then he nudged Buyu. They exchanged a strange look. Then they stepped back several paces. Skye frowned suspiciously, but she was distracted by Ord as it explored the mound, gingerly touching it with the sensitive suction cups at the ends of its tentacles. Finally, it rolled the end of one tentacle into a sharp spear point and pierced the mound. There was a hiss, as a horrible odor erupted from the wound. Skye hadn't thought anything could smell worse than the stink Ord had released in the tunnel, but this—it was worse. She screamed in disgust and scampered away, crashing into Zia in her haste to escape the stench. "Oh, help me," Zia moaned, falling dramatically to her knees. "Even Ord's farts don't smell that bad."

Upslope and upwind, Devi was half bent over with laughter, while Buyu wore a twisted smile, as if he were trapped between guilt and amusement. "You knew!" Skye accused. "You both knew Ord would pop open that stink."

"Sooth," Devi grinned. "I did some reading on mounds last night. They present some interesting questions."

"Yeah? Question this!" She scooped up a handful of humus and half-rotted leaves from the wet forest floor, and threw it at him. He dodged, and dove laughing behind a fallen log covered in green and brown moss. Skye raced up the slope with another clump of humus in hand and slammed it down on the backside of the log . . . then peered over to see the results of her work. But Devi was gone.

Uh-oh.

The counterassault fell before she could scramble away: a tall shrub leaning over the log started to shake violently, showering her in huge drops of water. "Gutter dog," she growled, swiping her wet hair out of her face.

It wasn't even noon yet, but she felt exhausted. Giving up, she sat down with her back to the log, looking at Ord as it balanced motionless on the mound, its tentacle jabbed deep inside the structure. Buyu was sitting on the ground drinking water and looking a little lost. Zia was pulling some rations out of his pack. "Here," she said. "Eat something." She tossed a packet toward Skye but it went wide. Devi's hand, gloved in olive-green, reached out to catch it with a sharp *smack*. He leaned over the log and handed it to her. "For you, my lady."

"Thanks."

His red and blond hair was dripping wet. It fell half across his face as he looked at her in concern. "Are you okay?"

"Sooth." She lied. In truth, she was feeling seriously tired, and a little dizzy. "You?"

He caught another packet from Zia and climbed over the log.

Then he sat down beside her. "I look at you sometimes, and I get a little scared."

"I look that bad?"

He smiled. "Hey Ord," he called. "Find anything?"

"Yes Devi. Many plague vectors and associated antibodies. Much Earth-based genetic data. Also, information storage systems and—"

"Have you found what we're looking for?" Devi interrupted.

"City library says yes."

At first Skye wasn't sure she had heard right. Then a hot flush of relief rushed out of her pores. She closed her eyes and tipped her head back against the log, realizing for the first time just how really scared she had been.

"Hey."

She opened her eyes and turned to look at Devi. With his long, wild hair falling over his tanned face, he did not look much like the mannered astronomer she had met on a rooftop just last night. He gazed into her eyes and he said, "You're okay. You understand? It's all going to work out."

She nodded, blinking back a sudden, frightening surge of tears. The lifeboats were out there, she was sure of it. And if Ord was right, then the Compassion plague they carried wouldn't be a threat to anyone anymore.

Chapter 12

*E*ver since the warden had been destroyed, Buyu had been in radio contact with the explorers stationed at the elevator column, assuring them his party was in no danger. Now he looked at Devi and said, "Another warden is on its way."

"It doesn't matter anymore." Devi's face was bright with a triumphant grin. "We've got what we came for."

Skye reached up to her shoulder to stroke Ord's tentacle. "Now comes the scary part. We have to tell city authority what we've learned."

"They won't want to listen to us," Zia said. "We're just dumb ados."

Skye thought about it. "You know, I think there's only one person we need to convince." She plucked Ord off her shoulder, holding the little robot in one hand like a doll. A smooth, gold, gelatinous doll, with a round head and tentacles for arms. Its body felt firm yet flexible, a water-filled cushion warm against her skin. "Ord, I want you to contact Yulyssa for me. Real time."

"Sure Skye. Then go home?"

"Sounds like a good plan to me."

Ord's face took on a look of intense concentration. Several seconds passed. Then its mouth opened. It spoke in Yulyssa's voice.

"Skye?"

She sounded worried. Skye realized she had never contacted Yulyssa in this way before. Quickly, she explained where she was, though she did not explain why. "Yulyssa, I need your help. I've learned something about my great ship, and it's of concern to everyone in Silk."

Skye expected an outcry, but Yulyssa's answer was calm. "Tell me."

"Not like this. I have to say it all at once or no one will listen. I want you to get me an audience with the city council."

This request silenced Yulyssa for several seconds. Skye imagined her accessing data bases, checking the news . . . or just thinking. Finally Ord's mouth moved again. "You're sure, Skye? The city council is not a forum for speculations. Unless you have something concrete, I don't think—"

"They'll want to know!" Skye insisted. "Trust me on this. Please."

Again, Skye listened to a long interval of silence. Then, "All right. I'll request an audience."

"As soon as we reach the city, okay? It would be dangerous to delay."

———

Sensei Matilé met them at the elevator terminus. Her hard-eyed gaze went straight to Buyu. "Buyu Mkolu, you have failed at your first duty as an explorer: to keep your clients safe."

"He has not!" Zia interrupted. "Buyu used the warden to distract the viperlion. Without his quick thinking, Skye might have—"

"Clients should never be permitted to approach dangerous wildlife." Sensei Matilé straightened her already-straight shoulders. "Buyu Mkolu. Your presence is required at an official inquiry this evening."

Buyu met her gaze, looking grim but determined. "Yes, ma'am."

"Unfortunately," Sensei Matilé continued, "the inquiry will have to wait until after an emergency council hearing. Buyu Mkolu, you have been summoned to testify, along with your clients. I am to escort you there. I don't know what's gone on today, young man, but I will find out."

—⁘—

Danger was a word the city council always respected. Every member had faced the unexpected rise of perilous events many times in their long lives. They had seen terrible things, and survived them. It was not in their nature to dismiss warnings, even if the warning came from an ado who was barely fourteen.

Skye sat with Devi, Zia, and Buyu, at a broad table in the council chamber. Ord fidgeted nervously, clinging to the table's underside. Ever since they'd boarded the return elevator, Ord had urged them over and over again to report to the monkey house. Skye tried to be patient. She explained why they couldn't, but Ord would not accept it.

As they had taken their seats in the council chamber, Ord crouched on the table, starting in again. "Please Skye. There are puzzle pieces in your sweat. Please go—"

She leaned forward, whispering fiercely, "If you mention the monkey house one more time, I'll give you to Zia to play with. I swear I will."

Ord fled beneath the table, though Skye could still feel the tap of its tentacles against her knees.

Like the others, she still wore her skin suit. Her hair was still soggy from the rain. And she was tired. She rubbed at her face with the palms of her hands, wishing she could just go home, go to sleep, deal with things tomorrow.

Impossible.

She looked up at the waiting council members. Six of the seven were already present. They sat behind a raised desk, staring down at the four ados who had summoned them. Two of them were actually present, in the flesh. The other four had come as ghosts—holographic projections—though they looked absolutely real. Skye knew they were ghosts only because she had seen them wink into existence instead of walking into the room.

One councilor looked annoyed at this sudden meeting. Most of the others seemed curious. Only Kona Lukamosch, the council president, appeared openly concerned.

Kona had been re-elected every year as council president ever since the city was settled. He was a large, well-muscled man, dressed in black, with long black hair fixed in tiny braids gathered in a neat ponytail at the back of his neck. Skye felt uncomfortable under his gaze, so she turned to look at the audience behind her.

There were seats for at least a hundred spectators, but so far only about twenty were taken. Yulyssa sat in the center of the front row, between Sensei Matilé and Devi's mother, Siva Hand. Behind them were Buyu's parents, surrounded by an entourage of aunts and uncles and cousins. Zia's mother and father had also come, though they were sitting (as usual) on opposite sides of the auditorium. Behind the family members, Skye recognized three mediots from some of the less popular news and gossip services.

Of course there was no telling how many of the city's six and a half million people would watch the video transmission of this hearing. Probably not many. Skye hoped it wouldn't be many. She pushed her wet hair out of her face with a nervous hand, just as a holographic projection of the seventh councilor winked on behind the raised desk.

"All present," council president Kona Lukamosch said. He was one of the two councilors who was not a ghost. His gaze fixed on Skye. "Skye Object 3270a."

"Sir."

"We've gathered here at the request of Yulyssa DeSearange, one of the city's most respected citizens. Yet Yulyssa was unable to tell us the subject of this session. Perhaps you could enlighten us?"

"Yes sir." She struggled against her fear and her misgivings. A rosy flush heated her cheeks. If she had a choice, she knew she would choose to disappear. She would give anything to be alone in her bedroom, waking up from a bad dream. But this was real, and it was about more than just herself and her own future.

She swallowed against a dry throat. Then she said, "Sir? I do ask that you let me make my full explanation, before you reach any judgment."

"Huh." It was a skeptical grunt. "We'll do what we must."

"Yes sir." She glanced at Devi. He nodded encouragement. Zia squeezed her hand. So Skye began her story in a voice that shook only a little. "As you probably know, I wasn't born here in Silk . . ."

At first she explained to them only what they already knew, that she had arrived in Silk on a lifeboat, that nothing was known of her past, and that it had always been assumed she was the lone survivor of a great ship destroyed by the Chenzeme.

"An accident happened yesterday that made me rethink that explanation."

She told of her bloody nose, and of what Ord had found when it performed a routine analysis of her blood. "In six days, maybe longer, I'll become contagious, capable of spreading Compassion plague to every adult in Silk. A day or two after that, I'll die."

Two of the council members sprang to their feet, demanding an explanation. Others, including Kona, looked thoughtful. Skye guessed they were linked through their atriums to the city library.

"There is no danger just yet," she said softly.

"According to your DI companion!" one of the councilors shouted. "Is it a medical specialist? I don't think so."

"It has contact with medical specialists," Skye said, her voice shaking a little more now.

Kona Lukamosch spoke next. "This room will be sealed until the status of this infection is confirmed." The audience murmured in outrage and fear, but Kona ignored them. He fixed Skye with a calculating gaze. "Please go on."

She nodded. "It occurred to us"—Here she glanced at Devi, Zia, and Buyu—"that my great ship might not have fallen victim to a Chenzeme warship after all. If Compassion plague was taking the lives of all the adults, it would only make sense for them to try to save their children—all their children—by putting us aboard lifeboats. We weren't sick. We wouldn't have shown any sign of the disease. So they would have no reason to think we were plague carriers too.

"It's true that no other lifeboats have ever been seen. I don't know why, but I do know they're out there. They have to be out there. I can't be the only one." She stared down at the table, where her gloved hand clawed at the cultured wood. Zia's gloved hand moved to cover hers, gold on blue. "The city council has never been interested in looking for other lifeboats. I was afraid you would refuse again, if you had reason to believe these other children were carriers of an incurable plague."

"We could never endanger the city," Kona said softly.

Skye looked up, startled by the unexpected sympathy in his voice.

"We have a duty to protect our own people," Kona added.

She nodded. "I know. That's why we took this trip today, down to Deception Well. Ord told us the monkey house had no cure for Compassion. So we went to the Well, to look for a cure—"

Here some of the councilors again interrupted, outraged, but Skye continued speaking, louder now, to rise above the protests.

"The Well is known to host hundreds of thousands of Chenzeme plague structures," she said. "Those that affect humans are concentrated in the mounds—"

"You cannot have touched the mounds!" one of the councilors cried, her voice cracking in fear.

"But I did," Skye said.

Again a chorus of protest erupted, but Skye kept speaking, determined to get through this: "Ord tapped a mound, and found a cure."

Then she repeated the claim to make sure everyone heard. "We found a cure! Ord found it. With the information Ord carries, the monkey house doctors will be able to synthesize a Maker that can eliminate Compassion plague. So even if every child from my great ship is a carrier, they won't be a danger to anyone here. Please listen to me! These children are real. They are human, and they are harmless, and it's the duty of every citizen of this city to look for them, and to rescue them." She shook her head. "If we don't help each other, then we might as well count ourselves the allies of our enemy, the Chenzeme."

—⁓—

Buyu spoke after that. Then Devi, and finally Zia. They all told the truth. None of them flinched in their opinions. The councilors asked questions, but even so, it was over quickly. Perhaps it was too much to expect an immediate decision, but Skye was disappointed just the same. She let Ord crawl up onto her hand again, taking some comfort from the slick touch of its curling tentacles. "Skye is sad?" it whispered.

"Just a little."

They were placed under arrest. A security officer escorted them to a temporary doorway newly opened in the floor of the council chamber. It was covered with a gel membrane. "This is a stairway down to a transit station," the security officer explained. "Proceed one at a time, and quickly board the waiting transit car."

Skye went first. She could not see the stairs through the white membrane, so she felt for them with her booted feet. Ord clung to her hand as she moved gingerly downward. The membrane squeezed at her ankles, then her legs, her hips, her belly, her chest. Finally she ducked beneath it and found herself in a narrow passage lined with more white membrane, though here it was thin, so she could see through it to the walls of the stairway. City authority was trying to keep any possible infection contained inside the membrane's walls.

Ord dropped from her hand and scurried ahead. "Monkey house now?"

"Sooth. No choice now."

She glanced back, but no one else had started down yet. So she hurried forward, following Ord. The membrane became a tunnel across an empty station platform. Its end kissed the open door of a transit car. Ord scurried inside, and Skye followed. Still no one appeared behind her. The door slid shut, the membrane withdrew, and the transit car pulled away. It didn't ask her where she wanted to go.

———

At the monkey house Skye was assigned to an isolation chamber. It was a comfortable-looking room, furnished with a sofa, a low table, a bouquet of flowers, and a sleeping pad. One wall was transparent. It looked out onto a small anteroom.

Skye jumped in surprise as a woman in a silver skin suit appeared suddenly beside the sofa. "Hello Skye. I'm Dr. Alloin." She smiled, but her eyes looked worried.

The doctor was present only as a holographic projection. She relied on a collection of robotic arms to do the medical work. The arms grew out of the wall as Skye watched: tiny hands and sharp needles on the ends of long, flexible cables. It looked creepy. Even Ord hissed, batting at the arms with its tentacles until Skye whispered, "It's okay." But her heart was racing.

The robotic arms pinched at her, and measured her temperature. They looked down her throat and into her eyes. They took her blood. They injected her with several painful jabs. Then finally, they went away. Dr. Alloin said, "We've uploaded the biochemical data from your attendant. While it's being analyzed, I'd like you to rest."

Skye nodded, as the doctor's projection vanished from the room.

A meal was sent, but Skye had no appetite. She felt horribly tired, as if all the energy in her muscles had drained away. Yet at the same time she did not feel sleepy. Something was waking inside her. She could almost feel it stirring, and it kept her awake. And afraid.

"Skye?"

She turned at the familiar voice, to see Yulyssa in the anteroom, on the other side of the transparent wall. Her dark hair was loose around her shoulders. Her eyes were soft with concern. Ord scurried up to the wall that separated them. "Skye is sad," it said softly. "Take her home now?"

Yulyssa's smile was faint. "Not yet, little one."

Skye said, "Yulyssa, I'm so happy to see you."

"Me too, love, though I wish you had come to me with this, before going down the Well."

"I was afraid. There was no known cure! And you know how the council is. Always so careful, so cautious, so wary. They would have required years and a thousand studies before they granted permission to check the mounds."

"It can seem that way sometimes." She looked around at the

empty anteroom. Then she shrugged, and sat cross-legged on the floor. "You were very lucky things turned out all right. The mounds are off-limits because they are dangerous. They can be a source of plague, as well as a source of cures. Your friends might have been hurt."

"I didn't do it just for me. You know that?"

"I understand."

Skye nodded, a simple movement, but it made her dizzy. She thought maybe she should lie down. So she dragged the sleeping pad to the transparent wall, then she collapsed on it, exhausted. She whispered, "I think it's starting, Yulyssa. I don't feel right anymore."

Chapter 13

For two days Skye hardly knew what was going on around her. A terrible fever trapped her in a world halfway between waking and sleep, where nasty dreams replayed over and over again. Now and then she wakened briefly, to find herself sweating and tossing on her sleeping pad beside the transparent wall. The lights were kept low. She found the semi-darkness a comfort as she lay naked beneath a thin sheet. She tried not to look overhead, where a swarm of robotic arms hovered like some gigantic spider, ever ready to measure her temperature, or sample her blood, or puncture her skin with an intravenous needle, or drain away her body's wastes.

Instead, she looked for Yulyssa, and Yulyssa was always there, lying on her side just beyond the transparent wall, her head propped on her hand, her dark eyes brooding, never sleeping. When she saw that Skye was awake, she would smile just a little, and touch her fingers to the barrier, so that Skye knew she would touch her face if she could. Skye longed for that touch. She thought she would die without it. She wanted it so badly that finally she found the strength to raise her own hand and hold it for a few seconds against Yulyssa's with only the barrier between them.

After that she slept a real sleep for the first time in two days, and when she awoke, she felt as if her body once again belonged to her. "Feeling better?" Yulyssa asked.

Skye smiled. "Yes." Then she added, "A war's been fought inside me, hasn't it? It feels that way."

"And the Chenzeme lost," Yulyssa said. Her eyes gleamed with joy. "Compassion plague has been defeated."

Skye had a fast, efficient metabolism, finely sculpted through many generations of genetic manipulation. Now that the Chenzeme plague was gone from her system, her body began to rapidly heal. After another long sleep she was able to get to her feet. She walked on wobbly legs to use the toilet while Ord followed nervously behind her. After that she sat on the sofa and brushed her short hair. It felt strangely heavy and oily.

"Some of your Makers have died off or gone dormant," Yulyssa explained. "They're not around to keep you clean."

Yulyssa spoke to the monkey house staff and a bath was sent to Skye's room. It rose up through the floor. Steam curled from the scented, slightly pink water.

"It's a nutrient bath," Yulyssa explained. "It will re-infect you with the Makers that you've lost."

Skye eased herself into the hot water and sighed in delight. Afterwards she dressed, then ate a small meal of soup and crackers. It was the first food she'd had in her stomach in days. It made her sleepy. She lay down on the sofa, her knees pulled up to her chest, stroking Ord's smooth tentacle as it curled around her fingers.

"Skye?"

"Mmm?"

"You have some visitors outside who would love to say hello."

"Really?" She sat up, looking at the doorway beyond Yulyssa. A moment later, Zia, Buyu, and Devi—with Jem balanced on his shoulder—crowded inside. Zia started to crack a joke, then her gaze fixed on Skye. Her grin faded. "Oh, *Skye*," she breathed.

"What?"

"I . . . it's just that I . . ."

"What?" Skye said, sitting up straighter. "Am I ugly?"

"Yes! Ado, I never saw anyone look so . . . *fleshless* before. It's like there's nothing between your bones and your skin. Your face, it's . . . like a skull. Look at your arms! There's nothing there."

Devi and Buyu looked just as shocked. *None of us has ever seen a person who's been sick,* Skye realized. She looked at her hands, her arms, her ankles. They *were* just bones draped in skin. It was as if her muscles and the thin, protective layer of fat that had wrapped her body had been melted away in the microscopic war that had raged inside her.

She felt suddenly ashamed. Especially with Devi and Buyu there. She must look hideous. Why hadn't Yulyssa told her? Skye looked for her, to demand an explanation, but for the first time in two days she did not see Yulyssa beyond the barrier. She must have slipped out to give Skye a few private minutes with her friends.

Her flash of temper faded. She flexed her hands, amazed that such bony things could still move.

"Hey," Devi said. "Just eat like Buyu for a day or two, and you'll be as good as new." His shock had passed. His smile was genuine.

"Sooth," Buyu said. "And maybe this time we'll really get Chef Carlisle."

Skye felt her shame seep away. She got up from the sofa, shuffled over to the barrier, then sat down heavily on the sleeping pad. Jem jumped off Devi's shoulder and nuzzled the transparent wall, trying to find a way into her lap. "Are you all okay?" she asked.

"We had some puzzle pieces in our blood," Devi said, crouching beside Jem and stroking the little dokey's back. "Ord figured it wrong. You were just becoming contagious, there in the council chamber. Almost everyone in the chamber was touched with it, but with us it was just getting started, so it was easy for the doctors to snip it out."

Skye could not think what to say to this shocking news. Ord had figured it wrong? Then she might have poisoned the whole city. She lay back against the pad and stared up at the ceiling. "I—I'm so sorry. I thought there was time. I—"

"You couldn't have known," Yulyssa said firmly. Skye turned her head, to find her standing just inside the doorway, her dark eyes cautious as she studied Skye. "Ord was right. Compassion should never have matured that quickly. The doctors are guessing something on the planet hurried its development. Deception Well is like that. You never know how the governors will react."

Skye looked away, as tears welled in her eyes. She had come so close, *so close* to causing a horrible disaster. The city might have died.

"Hey," Devi said. "It's not that bad. Even if you hadn't brought a cure back with you, Compassion would never have spread. We would have just gone into cold storage, and hibernated, while the monkey house docs worked up a counteragent. And if that didn't work, we would just grow our bodies over again."

"That's right," Yulyssa said. "The only way you could have harmed anyone was by denying you were sick, and giving the infection a chance to become widespread."

Skye didn't want to think about that. She wiped her eyes and turned to Buyu. "They kicked you out of the explorer corps, didn't they?"

Buyu could not quite meet her gaze as he shrugged. "They didn't have much choice."

"I'm sorry," Skye whispered.

Buyu's brows lowered in a fierce scowl. "Stop saying that, okay? We did what we did for a reason. I'd do it again."

"It was worth it," Zia agreed, "because we found a cure for Compassion."

Skye looked from Buyu, to Devi, to Zia, feeling a sudden bright hope stir under her heart. Zia was right. They had found a cure. "Then city authority is going to look for the lifeboats?"

The mood of her friends suddenly dimmed. Zia looked at her hands. Buyu frowned. Devi's eyes hardened in anger. "No," he said. "City authority is not going to look."

"But why not?"

"The same old reasoning," Zia said. "They say if there were other lifeboats, they would have shown up by now."

"And they say they've done surveys before," Buyu added.

"Not with radar," Devi growled. "They won't look with radar."

"But why not?" Skye asked, truly mystified.

Yulyssa stepped forward. "Because they're afraid. Strangers bring new ways, new diseases, new challenges. The city has been at peace now for as long as any of you can remember, but it hasn't always been that way."

Skye shook her head. "But if they're out there, they're only children. They need us."

Yulyssa nodded. "We still have to convince the council of that."

Chapter 14

Skye ate. Never in her life had she felt so constantly hungry. Never before had she consumed so much food. Her body used the calories for repairing and rebuilding her tissues. Day by day she gradually regained the weight she had lost, until once again she was sleek with muscle overlaid by a thin and healthy cushion of fat.

Only then did the doctors consent to let her out of the monkey house.

It was late at night, past midnight when she left. Skye couldn't understand why the docs had picked such an hour.

Yulyssa met her. There was no one else around. A transit car brought them home. All was quiet until they entered the courtyard of their apartment building, then they were set upon by a flock of camera bees. The buzzing machines swooped out from behind the shrubbery that flanked the building's entrance, startling Skye so badly she hissed and ducked away.

Yulyssa stood her ground. She glared at the camera bees, warning their operators in a voice that was deadly cold, "Leave now. We have nothing to say."

City law required they obey, or face harassment charges. The bees retreated, but they did not really leave. Skye could hear them buzzing within the shrubbery. "They want to talk to me, don't they?" she asked softly.

"Tomorrow," Yulyssa said, and they went inside.

In the morning the bees were gone, but only because Yulyssa had negotiated a media contract that required Skye to answer questions at an open press conference. The mediots were satisfied.

Siva Hand was not.

As Skye stepped outside, she was startled to discover Devi's mother waiting in the courtyard. Devi himself was not in sight.

Siva was dressed formally, with wide, stiff sleeves and deeply pleated pants. She stood with her back very straight. On her face was a look of impatient anger. One glance at Siva, and Skye felt as if she were late for a forgotten appointment. Nervously, she stroked Ord's tentacle as it curled gently around her neck.

The little robot had chosen to ride on her shoulder this morning. Now it murmured in her ear, "Scary lady, Skye. Go back. Go home. Yulyssa will help, yes? Please Skye?"

"Hush, Ord." Skye had to make this press conference. It would be her last good chance to persuade the city that she was not just some reckless kid. She couldn't turn back because Siva Hand stood in her way.

Of course she did not want a fight. So she decided to play dumb.

"M. Hand," she said, nodding her head in polite greeting. "You must have come to see Yulyssa. Do go on up. I know she'd love to receive you." And with that she tried to hurry past this woman who had lost her first family to a Chenzeme assault centuries before.

Something in Siva's icy voice made her stop. "Young lady, you know very well it's you I've come to see." This was not the same voice Siva had used that night Skye first met Devi. Then, Siva had seemed sweetly endearing. Now . . .

In her voice, Devi's mother carried the gravity of all the sad centuries she had been alive. Skye could not run from that voice anymore than she could have run from Yulyssa.

Siva watched her with eyes that were still and cold. "I've come to ask: Do you feel you have already caused enough pain for my family? Or do you plan still more? It has been only a few days since you forced yourself into my son's life, and yet his life is in ruins. Do you have some influence, beyond the influence of a wild little girl? Do have some special hatred for me? Have I somehow offended you, that you must steal away and ruin what I love most?"

Skye listened to this tirade, too stunned to interrupt. When she finally found her voice she spoke softly—but she could not have held back the words if they cost her life. "He's not your toy." Her anger was a hot red glow at the base of her mind, forcing her to speak. "He's not your special project."

"Oh sooth," Siva answered. "Divine is your project, isn't he? Under your guidance he has left his home and his studies. He has risked his life and endangered the city—"

"It's not like that! I didn't make him go—"

"Now you will tell me it was his idea."

"It doesn't matter whose idea it was!"

"I want you to stay away from him."

"Do you think that would make him come home to you?"

Siva flinched, as if Skye had slapped her. "You are a cruel child."

"Not as cruel as you! You cloned him from the son you lost, and all his life, all you've done is force him to *be* that son. But that's not who he is! That's not him!"

As soon as the words were out, she knew she'd said too much, but it was too late to take anything back. She looked at Siva's bloodless face and stuttered, "I- I'm sorry. I shouldn't have said that."

It was then she noticed Devi. He had come into the courtyard with Buyu. They must have come to meet her. Clearly, Devi had heard what she'd just said. He stood frozen beside Buyu, slack-jawed with surprise.

Siva turned to follow Skye's gaze, and smiled.

For several seconds no one spoke. Then Devi remembered to

close his mouth. He swallowed hard. Skye could actually see the anger flowing into his expression, displacing shock. "You had no right to say that," he told her, his voice soft and husky, like a growl. "You don't know anything about me. You don't know anything about my mother."

"Hey Dev," Buyu said, putting a massive hand on Devi's shoulder. "She didn't mean—"

Devi shrugged away from Buyu's touch and turned, leaving the courtyard at a swift walk that soon turned into a run. Siva's gaze settled once more on Skye. Pinned to her face was a small but triumphant smile.

Skye looked away. She felt so ashamed. She'd betrayed Devi. She wasn't supposed to know what she knew, and she certainly wasn't supposed to say it. But the words had popped out of her mouth and there was no way now to grab them back.

She wanted to run away. She wanted to hide. She wanted to lock herself in her room and cry. But the press conference would start in half an hour and she had to be there. It might be her last chance to persuade the city to listen. As if she could persuade anybody of anything.

"Hey," Buyu said. "You okay?"

It startled her to find him so close. He had bent down to look into her eyes. Siva Hand was gone.

Skye smiled weakly. "I have a big mouth, don't I?"

Buyu wisely chose not to answer that. "Give Dev some time to cool off." He hesitated. Then, "What did you mean about him being a clone?"

"It was something Yulyssa told me. I wasn't supposed to know. I shouldn't have said it. I should have let Devi tell me, in his own time."

But there was no way now to take it back.

Buyu walked with her to the little auditorium in the neighborhood of Vibrant Harmony, where Yulyssa had scheduled the press conference. Skye peeked in from a side door. She counted fifty-three mediots in the audience, all waiting to talk to her.

"Nervous?" Buyu whispered.

"Terrified," she whispered back. "But I might as well get it over with." She lifted Ord off her shoulder and set it on the floor. She didn't want the little robot crawling all over her, or asking silly questions while the conference was in progress. "Stay out of sight," she warned it. "Don't let anyone see you until I say it's okay. I mean it, Ord."

"Yes, good Skye." It scurried across the floor, then oozed beneath a potted plant and disappeared.

Skye drew a deep breath, touched palms with Buyu, then stepped inside.

Facing the mediots, she tried again to make the argument she had made before the council—that she could not be the only survivor of her great ship, that other lifeboats must surely be out there—but the mediots kept asking pointless questions. What had it been like to be chased by a viperlion? Just how bad did the mound really smell? Were fourteen-year-olds still children? Did she have sex in the forest?

Skye flushed, trying again and again to return the dialogue to the lifeboats, but no one wanted to talk about that. She felt like a parrot-bird muttering its memorized speech over and over, while no one listened. When it was over, she knew she had failed to persuade anyone that her cause was real.

Buyu and Zia met her outside the auditorium. "Hey ado," Zia said. "You did okay. They were just being twits."

True enough, but that didn't make her failure any easier to take. She felt hollow inside. What did she have left now? Devi was gone, no one would listen, and half the city thought she was a dumb ado taking crazy chances with everyone's life.

Zia tried to cheer her up, but what Skye really needed was time alone. After a while, she slipped away.

She went down to Splendid Peace Park, following a path that led to the little pavilion by the outer wall, where she and Devi had talked that first night. She had just reached the final bend in the path when a flash of purple and gold fur jumped out at her from behind a tree. She yelped, while the dokey sprinted over her feet, only to turn around again, grabbing her ankles with its tiny monkey hands, while its bushy tail waved in delight.

"Jem!" She knelt, running her fingers through the dokey's short fur. Then she froze. If Jem was here, then Devi . . .

She looked up, to see him standing in the path, watching her with troubled eyes. She flushed and looked away. "I'm sorry. I didn't know you were here. I'll go—"

"No. Stay for awhile. Please?"

She picked Jem up. Then she stood, cradling the dokey against her chest. "You're not angry?"

"Sure I am. I guess." He shrugged. "I'm angry most of the time these days."

"I'm sorry."

"How did you know?"

Her cheeks burned. "Yulyssa told me."

He nodded, as if he had already guessed as much. "I've got some fortune cookies. You want some?"

She wasn't hungry, but it was a nice excuse to stay. "Sure. I guess."

They sat facing the transparent wall of the canopy. By leaning forward just a little, Skye could look down on Deception Well's equatorial continent. *I've been there.* It was a fact she still found astonishing.

"Here," Devi said, lifting the lid on a small box covered in gold foil. "Have one. This is the forgiveness collection. I bought it for you."

The fortune cookies were golden discs arranged in two neat rows. Skye picked one up and turned it over. A message scrolled across the middle in chocolate-brown letters. It proclaimed *Obedience never requires forgiveness.* She wrinkled her nose and fed it to Jem.

Devi laughed. "Well, I haven't looked at them all yet. Here, try this one." He handed her another.

She held it, watching the chocolate words scroll past: I'm sorry I got angry . . . I shouldn't have walked out on you . . . Forgive me?

She looked up at him, amazed. "How did you do that?"

A rosy flush underlay Devi's brown skin. "Trade secret."

"You had a right to get angry." She nibbled at the edge of the cookie, while Jem batted the other one around on the pavilion floor.

"No," Devi said. "It was stupid of me. It's just that whenever I think about *him*—you know, my brother—I start to feel like . . . like maybe I'm not me. Only I'm not doing a very good job of being him, either. He could do almost anything."

"Sez your mom."

Devi smiled. He threw Jem another cookie.

"Anyway," Skye said, "we cured Compassion plague. That's something."

Devi grunted. "And if we could find those lifeboats, that would be something too."

Several seconds passed in silence. Then Skye felt a touch against her hand. She looked down, to see Devi's fingers resting cautiously on her own. "When you were sick," he said, "I was really scared. I've never been that afraid before. I've never met anyone like you."

Skye was in no mood to be impressed with herself. "Crazy and bad-tempered, you mean? With an out-of-control mouth?"

"Sooth. Exactly." Devi grinned. "And smart and tough too. And pretty."

His fingers closed around her hand. She felt a flush run through her, happy and fearful at once. She looked up, and it didn't surprise her at all when his lips touched hers in a tentative kiss. It felt soft and slightly wet, and silly, and essential all at once. It felt demanding, too, so that she had to trade a kiss with him a second time, and then a third.

She had never kissed a boy before. It alarmed her, the way that one simple gesture opened doors inside her that she had never dared to look behind. Frightened now, she pulled away. "I don't think—"

"No. It's okay." Devi breathed the words into her ear, sending a delicious shiver running through her. He pulled back a little and turned his head, getting ready to kiss her again.

She stood up abruptly. "I need to think about this."

He stared up at her, looking confused and a little angry. Then he drew a deep breath and nodded. "I understand. You're young."

Indignant now, she put her hands on her hips. "Right. Like you're an old fart." Then a new thought occurred to her. "How many girlfriends have you had?"

"One."

"One?"

"You."

Her eyes narrowed as she glared down at him. "I'm not your girlfriend."

He stiffened. He studied her for several seconds, as if trying to see the landscape inside her mind. Then he shrugged. "My mistake. I must have had a vision of our future relationship."

"That must be it." She moved a safe distance away before she sat down again. Not really sure why. Her skin felt hungry—that was the only way she could describe it—hungry to be touched by him, but at the same time something around her heart was afraid. *There's time*, she thought, and she left it at that, hoping Devi was willing to leave it alone too. For now.

After a minute or so of silence she said, "I'm not ready to give up on finding the lifeboats."

Devi had been staring down at the cloud patterns over Deception Well's coastal mountains, 300 kilometers below. Now he turned to her with an expression of surprise. "Of course not. But we aren't going to get city authority behind us unless we can explain why no other lifeboats have been seen. It really is an interesting question." He smiled, and she thought that maybe she had been forgiven.

"Let's start over again," he suggested. "Take a look at things from the beginning. Tannasen must have filed a detailed report on the discovery of your lifeboat. We need to pull that out of city library. We can go over it in detail, and maybe we'll turn up some clue suggesting why the lifeboats have been so secretive. Where's Ord?"

Skye realized she hadn't seen Ord for quite a while. She glanced around, then shrugged. "Somewhere . . . why?"

"Ord could do the library work for us. Hey Ord. Come here."
The little robot did not appear. "Ord?" Devi stood up, then circled
the pavilion, scowling into the bushes and frowning at the path.
Jem darted playfully around his feet. "Ord!" he called, louder now.
"Come here, okay? Ord?"

Still the robot did not show itself. Skye stood up too, alarmed
now. When was the last time she'd seen Ord? Some time before
the press conference. She hadn't thought to look for it, because
Ord always tagged after her. It never got lost. She ran a few steps
down the path, peering among the lower branches of the trees.
"Ord?"

"Maybe it was trapped in the building where you had the press
conference," Devi suggested.

"No way. It would just wait for a door to open, then it would
slide out."

"Maybe it did, but it couldn't figure out where you'd gone."

Was that possible?

She tried to remember the last time she'd seen Ord . . . and a
second later, she burst out laughing.

"What?" Devi demanded.

She laughed some more. Then, struggling for breath, she tried
to explain. "I warned Ord . . . to keep out of sight until I said it
was okay. It doesn't usually obey me this well." Skye knelt on the
ground. "Hey Ord, it's okay. Trouble's over and it's safe to come
out now."

The shrubbery rustled. Then Ord slid onto the pavilion. "Skye
is not eating right. Cookies are toy food. Come home to eat well,
good Skye."

Skye hardly heard the words. She stared at Ord, wrestling with
a sudden, terrifying thought. "Devi? I . . . I think I've figured it out.
I think I know what happened to the other lifeboats."

Chapter 15

*D*evi held Jem, scratching the dokey behind the ears as Skye
explained. "This is what we know about my lifeboat. It was
sighted when the solar sail began to grow. The sail was huge, like a
metal flag reflecting Kheth's light, very easy to see. Tannasen was
in command of *Spindrift*, and immediately he took the research
ship to investigate."

"Sooth," Devi said. "That's nothing new."

"What happened after that?" Skye asked him.

"Tannasen rendezvoused with the lifeboat, and found you."

"No. It was months before he reached the lifeboat. What happened next was, the solar sail started to shred. It was torn apart
when it hit pebbles in the nebula. It was set upon by butterfly
gnomes. Suppose the DI in command of the lifeboat mistook that
for an attack?"

Devi stared thoughtfully at Ord. "Then it might have warned
any other lifeboats behind it to stay quiet . . . just like you warned
Ord."

Skye nodded. "Their only defense is to go unnoticed."

"Ord stayed out of sight until you told it everything was okay."

"Sooth. Maybe the other lifeboats are doing the same thing—staying out of sight until they're told it's safe. But the DI on my lifeboat can't deliver that message because it isn't active anymore."

Devi put Jem down. "This is an interesting idea." He paced back and forth across the pavilion several times, his brow wrinkled in thought. "But something's missing. The DI must have some way to contact the other lifeboats. It would be senseless to send them into dormancy forever. But how could it send an all-clear signal if it's dormant too? It doesn't make sense . . . unless it's waiting for something . . . maybe for some kind of proof that things really are okay before—"

He stopped in mid-sentence, to stare at Skye. "It's you."

"What?"

"You're the proof. It's waiting for you. Think about it. Ord came only to your voice, not to mine."

"So . . . ?"

"Maybe the lifeboat is tuned to your voice as well. It would make sense. If you survived, then the others would stand a good chance too."

She shook her head. "I was only two! The lifeboat won't know my voice."

"Well, maybe it's not your voice. Maybe it's just you. Who you are hasn't changed since Tannasen picked you up. Not at the level of your cells. Not in your DNA."

"You think my lifeboat would recognize me?"

"Only one way to find out."

Her mouth went dry. "You aren't saying we should . . ."

Devi's gaze didn't waver. "That's exactly what I'm saying. We should make an expedition to your lifeboat, and see how it reacts."

"You're crazy. There's no way to get to the lifeboat. It's parked in the construction zoo. *In space.* Beyond the end of the elevator column . . . and the elevator column is tens of thousands of kilometers long. Tours don't run up the column, Devi. So how could we get out there? Were you thinking we could climb?"

He laughed. "If we did, we'd be old enough to be real people by the time we reached the end."

"So what do we do?"

He shrugged. "Well, if you like, we could ask permission to go up. Maybe city authority will finally get interested . . . but maybe not. And if they say no, you can bet they'll start watching us every minute. We got away with our excursion to Deception Well. If we give them any warning, we won't get away with anything again."

"So you want to sneak up there," Skye said softly. "Aboard an elevator car, I guess." There was no other way. She shook her head in wonderment. "Divine Hand, your mama is wrong. You're wilder than I am, by exponential powers."

———

Skye didn't see how they could ever find a way to sneak up to the construction zoo. To succeed they would have to slip past city security, stowaway aboard a restricted elevator car, and ride it all the way to the top of the elevator column without being detected. The journey would take days, and once there they would have to sneak off the elevator car, and somehow make their way to the construction zoo, where a great ship was being slowly assembled.

The construction zoo was not really a place. It was more like a gathering of parts and materials and pieces of the evolving great ship, along with the tentacled construction beasts known as lydras, a worker's habitat, and the lifeboat—all of it in orbit beyond the end of the elevator column. The trouble was that the zoo orbited at its own speed, and that was much slower than the speed at which the elevator column turned with the planet. So sometimes the zoo might be just a few kilometers away from the column's end, but at other times it might be ninety thousand kilometers away, on the other side of the world.

Whenever Skye asked Devi how they were going to get around all that, he just shrugged and said, "We'll work something out."

They spent the afternoon in the city library, going over every report ever filed on the lifeboat, learning as much as they could about its structure and capabilities. Tannasen's reports were not nearly as exciting as Skye expected. Mostly, they recorded position information, spectral analyses, radar profiles, communications attempts . . . she almost nodded off more than once.

Then she found Tannasen's personal journal. On the day the lifeboat was opened he had written, We have found a healthy baby girl. Nameless. Parentless. It is impossible to look on her sleeping face without wondering why. Why is she here? What miracle let her be found? We may never know.

There were also reports from the team of scientists who had examined the lifeboat after it was brought to Silk, and from a couple of researchers who had investigated it again during the intervening years.

By the end of the day they had uncovered two interesting facts.

First, the lifeboat was not the inert piece of abandoned equipment Skye had envisioned. Its life support system still functioned, so that even after twelve years in the construction zoo with no passenger to care for, it continued to maintain a livable habitat inside the pod. Even more intriguing, a researcher who had visited the lifeboat several years ago reported a surge of activity in the air filtration system during the first few minutes she was in the pod.

"That would make sense," Devi said, "if the lifeboat was trying to identify her. It could pull a few loose cells through the air filter, analyze them, and know whether or not this visitor was you."

The second interesting fact was that Tannasen and *Spindrift* were due to return to the city in only nine days. Devi's eyes sparkled at this news. Skye could guess why: "An elevator will be going up the column to carry supplies to the ship."

"Sooth," Devi said. "And we'll need to be on it."

Skye tapped her chin thoughtfully. "Devi? I think I'm getting an idea."

—⁓—

Skye's plan required Zia's help. That was a problem, because Skye didn't want to drag Zia into another mess. "Let her make up her own mind," Devi urged. "None of us are in this for the fun of it, Skye. What we're doing really matters."

So she set it up with Zia to meet them by the soccer fields in Splendid Peace Park. It was evening, and the clear canopy that enclosed Silk was pumping sunset colors over the city's slopes. The rosy light was reflected in the windows of the towering apartment complex of Old Guard Heights. Festival guns atop the heights fired pellets into the air that burst open into brilliant streamers that dissolved as they fell to ground, releasing delicious, tantalizing scents.

Skye and Devi wandered past the crowds of spectators gathering for the evening game, to an isolated stretch of lawn. Skye laid out a picnic blanket while Devi opened a basket of take-out food. Ord slipped out of it, melting around the edge of the basket.

Zia showed up a few minutes later. "So you two made up?"

Skye smiled. She was sitting cross-legged on the blanket. Devi was lying down beside her, watching the changing colors of the canopy. "For the moment anyway," Devi said.

Zia nodded. "I didn't think it would take long. So where's Buyu?"

Skye's smile faded. She exchanged a guilty look with Devi, while Zia's eyes narrowed. "You didn't tell him? Skye! He was really worried about you today."

Neither of them answered.

It didn't take Zia long to draw a conclusion. "Skye! You traitor. You're up to something, aren't you?" She glared at Devi. "You and the boy stargazer."

"Zia!"

Devi spluttered, trying to hide a laugh.

Zia wasn't amused. She cocked her head back, staring down the length of her nose at him. She looked ready to take someone apart. "What's going on, Skye? Tell me everything. Right now."

"Tell her," Devi urged. "Let her make up her own mind."

"Zia, you could get in trouble!"

"I've *been* in trouble! Sometimes it's worth it. But I hate it when people make decisions for me. Especially when they do it 'for my own good.'"

Skye nodded guiltily. "Sorry."

So. Nothing else to do now but talk. Zia would not shut up about it until she had the full story. "We need your help—"

"Wait," Zia said, holding up a hand. "Ord!"

The little robot peeped cautiously around the corner of the picnic basket, one tentacle winding around the handle like a vine.

Zia said, "Ord, order a message bee for me. Send it to Buyu. Tell him to meet us here."

"Message bee sent," Ord assured her, then it ducked out of sight again.

"All right, Skye. You were saying . . . ?"

"I was about to say that we need your help getting into the lydra house."

Zia's face relaxed a little. She sat down on the blanket, looking thoughtful. "Now why would you want to do that?"

Chapter 16

*L*ydras were artificial animals, designed to work in the zero-gravity environment of the construction zoo where the great ship was being assembled. They ranged from pocket-sized midgets to huge, tentacled construction beasts. Farmers like Zia's dad raised lydras in water tanks in the industrial levels beneath the city. Skye was interested in them because a cargo of freshly grown lydras was sure to be sent up to the construction zoo every time an elevator car made the run.

"We don't all need to go," Skye said as she pushed one of Ord's tentacles out of her face.

It was a few days later and she was dressed again in her electric blue skin suit. She carried a pack on her back, stocked with a few pieces of equipment and a generous supply of liquid nutrients—enough to fuel both herself and her skin suit for the next few days. She stood on a narrow transit platform deep inside the industrial levels of the inner city. It was an ugly place, hemmed in by gray walls and a low roof. Wide double doors bore the legend

"Adovna Lydra House - Entrance by Permission Only." Ord nervously patted her cheek.

Skye had told Yulyssa she was going to make an evening jump, and then spend the night with Zia. Zia had told her dad she was going to spend the night with Skye.

"Oldest trick in the book," Devi groaned when he heard about it. "Couldn't you be more original?" Easy for him to say. He was living on his own in Ado Town and didn't need to make excuses to anybody.

Buyu had put on a superior look. "I moved out, too. Of course, it's the third time I've gotten my own place, so nobody's too worried about it. My dad says I'll give up and come home again in a few days."

They had all laughed as they crammed together in a single transit car, but their mood had turned serious when the transit car's DI asked them their destination. "Adovna Lydra House," Zia had said stiffly.

"Adovna Lydra House is a restricted area," the car replied in a softly troubled feminine voice.

"We have a pass." From a pocket of her gold skin suit Zia produced a key card she had borrowed from her dad three days before. She had used it to take them on a tour of the lydra house, and then had held on to the key instead of returning it. Her dad asked about it once, but a shipment was going out, and he had a lot on his mind.

Zia slipped the key card into a slot on the transit car's console. Skye stared at her gloved hand: it was shaking. "You okay, Zia?"
"Sure."

The key card was good for five days.

"Your entry is approved," the car said warmly as it pulled away from the transit station, accelerating smoothly along its track. "We will arrive at Adovna Lydra House in four point two minutes."

The journey had seemed faster than that. Now they stood on the industrial station fronting the lydra house, watching the car slip smoothly away through the gel membrane that sealed off the airless transit tunnel.

Skye looked around at her friends, determined to try one last time to persuade them to rethink what they were doing. "We don't all need to go," she insisted. "In fact it's silly. If this plan works, then I'm the only one who really needs to reach the lifeboat."

"Sure," Zia said. "But you could get into trouble along the way."

"You could need help working through a problem," Devi added.

Buyu started striding toward the double doors, his pack swaying on his back. "Face it, Skye," he called over his shoulder. "We'll get in just as much trouble for knowing about this little adventure as we will for going along—so we might as well go along, right? We planned it that way."

"You're all crazy!" Skye told them—not for the first time. Then she smiled. "But I'm glad you're with me. Okay. Let's go."

It was early evening, though there was no way to tell that in the windowless passages of the industrial levels. The farmers who worked in the lydra house had gone home hours ago, including Zia's dad.

Now Zia used her key card to open the doors. A gush of cold air washed over them. At first, the interior looked absolutely dark. Skye was surprised. When they'd visited before, the lights had been dim, but it had been easy enough to see. She shuffled in behind Zia, holding onto her shoulder. The doors closed behind them, and for a moment she could see nothing. It reminded her of the lava tube. She listened to the trickle of circulating water. A pungent scent lay thick upon the air.

Ord hissed in her ear. "Nasty things here, Skye. Bad news. Go home?"

"Not yet," she said, stroking the tentacle that coiled around her arm.

Zia said, "The lights go down after the farmers leave, but it's not completely dark."

Indeed. As Skye's eyes adjusted, she could make out cold points of light overhead, like a projection of the thin starfield visible from Silk. The false starlight glittered faintly against the surface of a rectangular pool nearly as big as a soccer field. Water trickled into it at several points around its edge. This was lydra pond number 1. Something slapped the surface of the water, and Skye jumped.

"Whatever you do," Zia said, "don't fall in the water."

As her dad had put it, lydras were construction beasts, and they were always looking for something to do.

Zia took the lead. The others followed her single file around the edge of the pool. It felt like a long way. Twice Skye tripped over something that slithered away from her foot. "Zia, I thought lydras were supposed to stay in the water?"

"And we're supposed to stay in Ado Town," Zia said.

"You mean they can crawl out?"

"Only the little ones. The big ones weigh too much. They need the buoyancy of the water to hold them up. That's why they're raised in ponds."

Lydras in the Adovna ponds ranged in size from seed stock only a few cells in size to juvenile specimens two meters across. Earlier today, the juveniles in pond 1 had all been harvested. They'd been sprayed with a chemical solution that sent them into a state of hibernation, and then they'd been packed inside shipping containers. In just over an hour the containers were scheduled to be loaded aboard the next elevator bound for the top of the column.

As they rounded the far end of the pond, Skye made out the shapes of the white shipping containers, lined up in a row beside a warehouse door that would open onto a cargo bay.

Zia reached the first container: a box as tall as her chest and three meters long. She touched the locks on its upper surface. They opened with a smooth click. Skye and Devi crowded in close beside her as the lid slid back.

At first Skye could see nothing. Then Buyu produced a flashlight. The beam fell on a mass of wet tentacles, glistening in a spectrum of colors from red to blue to green and purple. Skye felt her stomach squeeze tight. Ord hissed again and crept around behind her neck.

"Last chance to turn back," Devi said in a low voice.

Zia giggled. "We'll be okay. Really. Because they're dormant. Look." With her gloved hands she picked up a pink lydra from the top of the heap. It was a bundle of tentacles arranged around a disc-shaped body, with small eyestalks sprouting between the limbs. Zia lifted one tentacle after another, then let it fall. The lydra did not respond. "They'll stay dormant until they're hosed down, or until the chemical wash evaporates in hard vacuum. So we'll be fine. Now let's make some room in this box before the cargo handlers get here."

The plan was to dump some of the lydras back into the pond so that the four of them could fit inside the shipping container. Skye wished they could dump all the lydras, but the weight had to be right. They could take out only enough animals to balance their own mass.

She slipped her gloved hands into the box. Ord shivered. "Bad job, Skye."

She couldn't argue.

Lydras looked as if they ought to be soft and squishy like Ord, so when Skye touched them, she was surprised to discover they were not. "Hey, they feel hard."

"That's because they're engineered to live in space," Devi said.

She picked up a green lydra with tentacles the length of her forearm, and held it in the thin beam of Buyu's flashlight. Peering closely, she could see that its body was armored in thousands of tiny scales. When she ran a hand along one of the tentacles, it felt as if it were encased in a shell, and yet it bent easily. Her skin suit was designed the same way.

It made sense. The pressure of vacuum would destroy the body of any ordinary animal, but the lydra's scales acted like the hard walls of a space ship, maintaining air pressure inside their bodies. When the lydra needed to move, the scales slid smoothly past each other, allowing the tentacles to bend. "It feels nice," Skye said. Like a toy that could be set in any posture.

Zia had disappeared into an equipment alcove. Now she returned, pushing a bin set on wheels. "Fill this up," she ordered. "It'll give us the weight of the lydras, then we can dump them in the pond."

They worked quickly, moving the hibernating lydras from the

huge shipping container into the smaller bin. Most had tentacles less than a meter long, but Skye discovered an orange-colored specimen with tentacles almost twice that length, each one as thick as her lower leg. She and Zia worked together to lift it, but it was too heavy. Zia frowned. "I wonder how one this large was overlooked in the last shipment?" Buyu came over to help but Zia shook her head. "Leave it. It's so big, that it's probably started to feed on the smaller lydras. If it doesn't get shipped out tonight, it could cause a lot of problems in the juvenile pond."

Skye frowned at the orange lydra. She wasn't eager to share the cargo container with such a monster. Zia saw the look on her face and grinned. "Stop worrying! It's sedated."

"Worry?" Skye said. "Me?" She shoved an orange tentacle back over the rim of the box. It hit with a wet slap against the tangle of dormant lydras. "Doubt never enters my mind."

"Oh sooth. I believe you."

When the bin was loaded, they noted the weight, then wheeled it to the edge of the pond. Zia ordered the bin to tip. Illuminated in the flashlight beam, the lydras splashed into the water. For several seconds they sank, drifting helplessly toward the shadowed bottom. But just before they passed out of sight, Skye saw a few of them stir. Tentacles snapped, and several young lydras shot off into darkness. "It didn't take them long to wake up," she said softly.

Zia threw a companionable arm around her shoulder. "Hey ado, we could ask city authority for permission."

Skye grimaced. "That's all right."

"I thought you'd feel that way." She ordered the bin back to its storage room. "Okay. It's time for the next step: Load the humans."

Skye felt her stomach knot. Jumping off the elevator column was exciting. Getting chased by a viperlion was exciting. Testifying in front of the city council was exciting. But climbing into a box full of tentacled carnivores . . . that was crazy.

Zia went first. Then Buyu. They nestled down among the dormant lydras, grinning like it was fun or something. "Aren't you going to put your hoods up?" Skye asked.

Zia shrugged. "Think we should?" She smiled as her hood rolled up over her head and across her face. Buyu also sealed his suit.

Devi turned to Skye. "You okay?"

"Sure."

He touched her face with his gloved hand and smiled. Then his own hood rolled up and sealed. He climbed into the container.

Skye reached up to stroke Ord. "Remember what to do?"

"Yes good Skye," the little robot whispered. "Seal the container." "Then?"

"Slide like spit down the side" —Skye grimaced as Ord echoed exactly Zia's stern instructions— "then crawl under the container. Spread thin and stick like gold mold to the container's underside. No motion and no noise allowed!"

"Okay," Skye said. She lifted Ord from her shoulder, and set it on the ground. "One more piece of advice: Watch out for crawling lydras."

She shrugged her hood on. Then she reached around to the bottom of her backpack, checking for the tube that carried liquid nutrients to her suit. It was firmly in place, in a socket above her hip. So she climbed the container, leaving Ord squatting on the floor, its head rotating from side to side as it searched the dark for crawling monsters.

For several seconds, Skye crouched on the container's rim, gathering her nerve. Devi, Zia, and Buyu had wriggled down into the mass of lydra bodies. They were buried to their chins, and the box appeared nearly full again. *Just room enough for me.*

Too bad.

Skye let her feet slide in first. She forced her legs down between the stiff, slippery tentacles. Then she lowered her torso, wriggling hard to slip her pack past the dormant lydras, trying not to think about where she was or what she was doing.

Through the visor of his hood she saw Devi's eyes, watching her. She suspected he was grinning. She wanted to say something nasty but her throat was too dry. So she ignored him, working her way down among the slick tentacles until she'd buried herself to her hooded chin.

Ord had climbed onto the rim of the box. Skye saw its slim, graceful tentacles reach for the switch that would close the cover. Zia's voice arrived over the skin suit's radio system. "Okay ados. This is it. All the way under so Ord can close up."

Buyu chuckled. "This is the weirdest thing I've ever done." Then he wriggled back and forth until he disappeared beneath the lydras. Zia and Devi copied him, vanishing in turn. Skye waited until Ord triggered the closing switch. Then she jiggled and thrashed, driving herself under the surface as the cover slid shut, cutting off the faint, false starlight of the ceiling.

For a moment, she could see nothing. Then she noticed a dim, jewel-like glow in many colors, bleeding through the packed lydra bodies. "Buyu, is your flashlight on?"

"Can you see it?"

"I can see lots of colors."

"Everybody okay?" Zia asked.

"Sooth."

"Sooth."

Skye added her own reluctant agreement. "Should have brought a patch to make me sleep."

They laughed, then Zia said softly, "We should be quiet now. It won't be long before the cargo handlers arrive."

So Skye tried to relax—as if that were possible, packed into a container full of sleeping monsters. In the faint gleam of Buyu's light she thought she saw one of the tentacles twitch. She stared at it a long time, waiting to see if it would move again.

Chapter 17

The elevator car shot upward along its track at 650 kilometers per hour . . . but the elevator column was more than 38,000 kilometers long. The journey to the top would last two and a half days.

Skye thought about this as lydras pressed against her on every side. She listened for the cargo handlers, hoping the robotic machines would come soon to load the container aboard the elevator car.

The plan was to spend only a few hours boxed in with the lydras. Once the container was loaded and the elevator car underway, Ord would release them. After that it would be a matter of staying out of sight. That shouldn't be too hard. According to Zia's dad, only five to ten human technicians would be aboard the elevator car. And since the car was the size of a small building, there would be plenty of places to hide.

They would have an easy time of it too, because security in Silk was never tight. Usually, it didn't need to be . . . though Skye could see how that might soon change. She felt badly about it.

But this isn't about me!

What they were doing didn't feel truly right. Still, it was the best choice she could see. Skye had to follow her conscience. If there were other children from her great ship—and she could not doubt there were . . . maybe she even had brothers and sisters somewhere?—she owed them her best effort. The laws of Silk did not have the moral authority to make her turn away.

A sudden loud *thunk!* against the side of the container brought her back to the present. She heard a faint mechanical whir, then the box shook. *At last!* The robotic cargo handlers had begun to move the lydra crates.

Inside the box, everyone (and everything) stayed very quiet. Skye strained her ears, trying to guess what was happening outside, but few noises could get past the triple barrier of her hood, the lydra bodies, and the wall of the cargo container. So it surprised her when the box was set down with a clunk. Were they on the elevator car already? It must be, yet the brief journey from the lydra farm had been so smooth she'd hardly been aware of it.

A louder clunk resounded through the container as something pounded down against the top. Skye cringed, listening to the walls creak and groan. She half-expected the box to shatter, but nothing happened.

After that she heard only a few distant thuds, followed by a blind silence. She thought about Ord, melted against the bottom of the container. She hoped it was all right . . . and not just because she was fond of the little robot. There would be no way out of this box if Ord could not trigger the locks.

———

It should have been impossible to sleep surrounded by lydras, yet sometime later Skye stirred, realizing she'd been dreaming. Now her eyes opened on perfect darkness. She could feel the pressure of lydras all around her and her heart raced. "Time?" she whispered to the DI that controlled her skin suit.

The answer wrote itself across her visor in glowing letters. Four hours had passed since they'd climbed into the lydra box. So the elevator must be underway, rushing along its tracks at 650 kilometers per hour as it left Silk and Deception Well behind.

Was anyone else awake? She activated her suit's radio, engaging a low power, private link to the others. "Hey, ados." At first she whispered, but then she said it again in a louder voice. "Hey! Ados."

"Skye?" That was Zia's voice, sounding a little confused.

"Sooth, it's me. Think it's too early to get out of here?"

"Wha' time . . . ? Oh."

"It's probably okay," Devi said, sounding fully awake, and annoyingly alert. "Either this storage room is empty, or it's never going to be empty. The only way to know is to look."

"We could radio Ord," Buyu said. "Let the little 'bot take a look for us."

Skye felt stunned at this excellent suggestion. A moment later she started to giggle. "I . . . I don't think so."

"Why?" Buyu demanded.

She knew she was being rude. She tried to stop laughing, but the situation was *so* ridiculous. She struggled to choke out an answer anyway. "It's just . . . I just realized . . . Buyu, I've never called Ord before, and I . . . I don't have any idea how to do it."

"Gutter dogs."

"Sorry."

"I've called Ord," Zia said quietly, "but I always went through city library. We can't do that here."

"We'll tap on the floor," Devi said. "That'll wake Ord up. It's smart enough not to show itself if anyone's around. Right, Skye?"

Ord was only a DI. "I don't know. Maybe."

"Try it," Zia said. "No choice."

So Devi knocked at the bottom of the container with his booted heel. They waited. Skye tensed, as she heard a scuttling sound, climbing the outside wall of the container. "Listen! Ord's coming."

They waited a full minute, but they heard nothing else.

"Maybe it sighted someone," Zia whispered.

So they sat quietly for most of an hour. In all that time they heard nothing, so finally Devi knocked again on the bottom of the container. They heard the scuttling again, but this time it came from the top of the box, near the locks.

"Ord's out there," Devi said. "Skye, can you rap the wall on that side?"

She was sitting beneath the locks, on the side of the container that would open first "I'll try."

Forcing a hand up, she pushed through the slippery lydras, trying to reach the top of the box. Her fingers had just touched the lid when a lydra tentacle snapped past her hand, shooting over her palm like a cool, wet, *living* rope. She yelped. "It moved! One of the lydras is awake."

"It can't be awake," Zia said. "It was probably just a reflex." Yet she sounded unsure.

"*Zeme twice*," Skye whispered. Her heart was pounding so hard she thought she might choke on it. She reached again for the top of the box. Making a fist, she pounded on it, lightly at first, then a little harder.

"That's enough," Devi said. "If Ord's there, it'll know we want out. It'll let us out, if things look safe."

They were silent for several seconds. Then Buyu said, quite calmly, "I can feel a lydra moving against my chest."

Skye let out a little scream. She couldn't help herself. Quickly, she closed her eyes and counted to ten, struggling against panic.

Through her skin suit she felt a tentacle wriggle under her armpit. Another coiled around her ankle. The skin suit was very sensitive. It was designed to reproduce sensation. She could feel the tentacle's tiny pincers plucking at her leg. "Something's going very wrong," she whispered.

"Sooth," Zia said. "I think it's our body heat. It must be wiping out the effect of the hibernation drug. Let's get out of here now." She clicked off her radio system, then raised her voice in a shout that Skye could hear easily, even through the hood of her skin suit. "Ord! Key the locks right now, or I am going to melt you when I do get out of here!"

The tantalizing scuttling started up once again. Then to Skye's heartfelt relief, she heard the locks click open overhead.

She waited, but the lid did not slide back. "Ord?" she whispered, forgetting for a moment that Ord could not hear her.

"What's going on out there?" Devi demanded. He grunted, and the container rocked a little.

"Are you trying to push the lid open?" Skye asked.

"Sooth."

She resolved to help him. Reaching for the lid, she forced both her hands past the lydras—until a flash of searing heat across one palm made her cry out. She yanked both hands back against her sides, breathing hard. Her skin suit felt hot. The seared glove was stiff. She could hardly bend that hand.

"Don't panic," Zia said.

"I'm not panicking! But something's going on here. My skin suit's heating up. It's not flexing."

"The lydras are trying to dissolve our suits," Devi said. "It's what they do—process raw material into something useful."

"I don't think I like your definition of raw material. Can they get through the suits?"

Devi didn't answer. Skye decided that was as good as a yes. Ignoring the stiffness in her palm (it was spreading to her arms), she reached overhead again and found the lid. It was designed to slide open. She ran her hands across it, feeling for some bump or ridge that she could grip, but the surface was absolutely smooth. Reaching back over her head, she found the seam where the lid met the side of the box, but it was a perfect fit. There was no way to get her fingers around the edge. "Devi—"

"I know, I know. I can't get a grip either."

"Then what are we—" She caught herself. "We *are* dumb ados," she growled. "The gloves of our skin suits are hot zones, remember? Zia, they bond to the elevator column when we swing in from our jumps. Why can't they bond to the lid of this cargo box?"

"Skye," Devi said, "you are a genius." He whispered to his DI. She whispered to hers, but the news was bad. "My gloves are disabled. The lydras have done something to them—"

"Mine are working," Zia said.

"Mine too," Buyu added. "I wish I was at the front of this box though. The lid's going to slide away on this side, and I'll have to readjust my grip. But let's try it. Devi, you ready? On three. One, two, three."

Skye felt the lid snap back a fraction of a millimeter, but that was all. The radio spat out a chorus of groans and curses.

Why wasn't the lid sliding open? It had opened so easily when they were in the warehouse.

A horrible, scraping noise erupted overhead. A knife of colorful light plunged into her eyes. She ducked her head, blinking hard. Then she looked again.

Between the packed lydra bodies a crack of light streamed into the box. "It's opening!" she shouted. Then she shoved the wriggling lydras aside so she could see better. To her disappointment, the gap was only a centimeter wide. "Well, it's opening a little."

The outside light was amber. As she reached for the crack, Ord's tentacle—stretched to the thinness of a noodle—wriggled into sight. Skye smiled, imagining the worried mutters of the little robot. *Skye is stuck. This is not fun . . .*

Time to get un-stuck then. She shoved her fingers into the gap and pushed. The scraping sound grew louder as the lid moved, first two centimeters, then three. Then five. Then ten. But the line of amber light did not widen at all. "Stop!" Skye yelped. "Stop, stop. Something's wrong. Something's out there."

She could feel a new bloom of heat at her knee. She thrashed, trying to get away from the lydra that wanted to dissolve her. Tentacles were wriggling on all sides now. Her glove had hardened into a cast. The elbow of her skin suit was going stiff too. She jammed her fist through the gap anyway, while Zia demanded, "What? What is it?"

"Something's been stacked on the lid." She pushed against it, as Ord's tentacle wrapped affectionately around her wrist. "*Gutter dogs.* It's really heavy."

Zia groaned. "Another container! Zeme dust! They've stacked the containers, and now we're trapped in here."

"No," Devi said. "It's not that bad. Buyu! Get over to this side of the box if you can."

Skye felt herself bounced around as Buyu and Devi stirred waves in the massed lydras. Buyu bashed into her, driving her up against the container's wall. She grunted and wriggled out of the way, only to run into Devi on her other side.

"Okay, Dev," Buyu said. "I'm in place, but there's no way we can lift this much weight."

"It's not that much weight anymore," Devi said. "Think about it. We're four hours out of Silk. That means we're twenty nine hundred kilometers above the surface of the planet."

"So?"

"Gravity is caused by the planet's mass, right?"

"Sure."

"The force of gravity drops rapidly the farther we get from its source. When we were on the planet, didn't you feel a little heavier than in the city?"

"I thought that was just the humidity."

"It wasn't. And this far from the planet, the pull of gravity might be only half what it is in Silk. We might not be able to move a loaded container in Silk, but I bet we could handle it here, where it weighs only half as much."

"Do it quick," Skye pleaded. "My skin suit's freezing up."

"Okay," Buyu said. "Ready? On three. One, two, three—!"

Devi roared. Buyu groaned. Skye laid her own stiff hands against the container that imprisoned them and strained, while waking lydras wriggled out from under her feet.

The massive container began to move. Skye felt it rise slowly, slowly up. Five centimeters. Ten. Amber light blazed through the widening gap while sweat popped out all across her skin. She could feel Buyu beside her, his huge muscles trembling. She pushed harder, and suddenly something snapped. She heard it as a metal *twang*.

The reluctant container started to slide. Devi roared again. Buyu howled. His huge arms surged over Skye's head, tipping the imprisoning container up, up out of her reach. Skye wriggled past the partly opened lid of their own box. She had to slip out of her pack to do it, hauling it out behind her by its strap. She emerged in time to see the defeated cargo container begin a graceful plunge.

It slid over the side of their container, falling as if in slow motion. It seemed to take a long time to reach the floor, but when it did, it hit with a horrible crash.

Suddenly, lydras were bouncing everywhere. "Oh no!" Skye screamed. "The lid must have broken!"

She shrugged her pack back on, then heaved herself onto the rim of their container. She balanced on top of it, one foot on the rim, one on the lid while she took in their surroundings.

They were in a huge warehouse, fully the size of one floor of the elevator car. Narrow aisles divided stacks upon stacks of containers of all shapes and sizes. Their own cargo container had been placed alongside an aisle. Skye gazed down three meters to the floor. The fallen container blocked the walkway. The concussion had cracked it open, sending hundreds of lydras careening into the air—blue ones, red ones, green and orange—flying wildly in the low gravity, crashing into the ceiling, and into other containers, before finally falling back down. Skye ducked, to avoid being hit by a circle of plummeting tentacles. Below her, the aisle writhed with lydras that had crawled or spilled from the overturned box.

It took only that quick glance to realize just how lucky they were.

Their container was in the middle of what had been a stack of three. If they had been on the bottom of the stack, they never would have been able to push two cargo containers over. If they had been placed anywhere but along an aisle, they never would have gotten the top container to tip. So they would have been stuck with the waking lydras for three days. It made her stomach clench, to think about it.

"Watch it, Skye," Buyu warned. "I can't fit through this crack."

He didn't give her any time to respond. He just shoved the lid open.

"Hey!" Skye yelped as she lost her footing. She teetered for a second on the edge of the cargo container. Then she felt herself falling. "Buyuu!" she howled, as she plunged back into the box from which she had just escaped.

Chapter 18

"Come on, Skye," Buyu complained as he stood on the rim of the box looking down at her. "Stop fooling around."

Fooling around?

Skye's gloves were so stiff she could not bend her fingers. She was covered in wriggling tentacles, her skin suit felt like it was on fire, she couldn't reach anything solid with either hands or feet, and Buyu was accusing her of fooling around?

"Help me get out of here!" she screamed at him. "Buyu! Or you are a dead man."

Someone caught the half-curled fingers of her rigid hand. She twisted around and saw that it was Devi. He had a wicked gleam in his eyes as he hauled her across the writhing lydras. "That was a beautiful dive, Skye! Wish I'd caught it on record. Have you ever thought about working with lydras professionally . . . ?"

She glared at him, silently vowing to get even. It didn't take long. As she reached the rim of the cargo container, she kicked the last of the clinging tentacles away. Then she hooked her stiff fingers around the rim and launched herself headfirst out of the box, driving her shoulder into Devi's gut as she did it.

Devi was so surprised that he was still holding her hand as they flopped together over the side.

Too late, Skye remembered it was a full three meter plunge to the floor. She got her forearms in front of her to take the brunt of the fall. At least the gravity was half normal! So she didn't hit as hard as she would have in Silk, but it was hard enough. The air was knocked out of her lungs, so it took her a few seconds to realize she had landed on a writhing cushion of lydras. After that she was on her feet in an instant, scurrying back up the stack of containers to get away from the beasts while Devi lay on the floor laughing uproariously.

Skye ignored him. She had a new worry. Among all the tentacles, she did not see any slender gold ones. What had happened to Ord?

"Unseal my hood!" she shouted at her suit's DI. The hood unfurled. She looked wildly around. "Ord? Ord where are you?"

"You dumb ados!" Zia shouted, glaring at them from atop the stack of containers. "Stop fooling around and get out of sight! That crash must have been heard through the whole elevator car. The crew is going to be checking out everything through the security cameras. Buyu, help me get this container closed. Hurry!"

Hurry? Skye had a sudden hollow feeling in her chest. It was over, wasn't it? "Zia, when they see this mess, they'll know we're here."

"Maybe, maybe not," Zia snapped. Working together, she and Buyu slammed shut the container's lid. Buyu punched the locks. "Maybe they'll think the containers were stacked wrong," Zia said. "Now *hide*."

"I have to find Ord. Ord!"

At last she heard its whispery voice from across the aisle: "*Skye, this is not fun.*"

"Ord." As she watched, it emerged from a narrow gap between two shipping containers. At first she could only see its head. Then a delicate tentacle slipped into sight. Skye held out a hand. "Swing over here. I'll catch you."

The tentacle stretched across the aisle to wrap around Skye's wrist. As Ord oozed out of the crack its body was as flat as a sheet of heavy gold cloth. It started to regain its shape as it swung over the gap, but it still looked partly crushed as Skye boosted it to her shoulder.

"Now hide!" Zia commanded.

Devi had climbed back up. So together they scurried over the closely packed cargo containers, dropping one by one into holes or gaps between the boxes. Skye was the last to find a hiding place. She jumped down into another aisle, then squirmed feet first into the gap beneath an angled container.

"Go home now, Skye?" Ord whispered.

"Shh! Don't talk."

It was quite likely they had already been seen through a security camera.

Maybe not, though.

She lay in silence, listening to the squirm and thump of the lydras loose in the next aisle. It sounded as if they were climbing the crates, only to fall back with wet *thumps*.

Time crawled past. She counted her breaths, but got bored before she reached fifty. She decided to take a look at her glove. Her palm was encrusted with a layer of smooth, white pseudoceramic, like the stuff most of the containers were made of. The lydras must have excreted it, obeying some programmed construction instinct. She picked at the layer, and it flaked off, bit by bit. Her skin suit was discolored beneath it, but the suit was self-repairing. Given a few minutes, it should be able to fix itself, just as her own body could quickly heal an injury.

The sound of footsteps shattered these idle thoughts. She held her breath, listening. The footsteps came from the other side of the warehouse. A woman said something Skye could not understand. Another woman spoke more clearly, "Zeme dust. What a mess!"

In a deep voice, a man demanded to know, "How could this happen? The containers were strapped together."

The first woman answered, "If the load's unbalanced, it will fall. We're going to have to run checks on the cargo handler that stacked this shipment. The program may be decaying."

Skye listened to them talk, relieved to hear them blame the loading equipment for the accident. Not once did anyone suggest a trespasser might be aboard the elevator car. And after all, why should they suspect such a thing? People in Silk did not sneak aboard restricted elevator cars, or take off to investigate the forbidden communion mounds. Of course Skye wasn't really from Silk. What had Yulyssa said? Strangers bring new ways, and new challenges.

The chatter went on for most of an hour as the elevator crew sprayed the escaped lydras with more of the chemical solution that sent them into dormancy. Then they gathered them up and repacked them. Jammed into her little hidey-hole, Skye was stiff and cramped by the time the voices retreated to the far end of the warehouse, and faded away.

She waited ten more minutes. Then she crawled out and stretched, working some blood back into her limbs. Ord crept out behind her. "Not a good house for you," it observed.

Skye nodded somberly. "I agree."

She climbed the stacks, to find Devi and Zia emerging from separate holes. Buyu appeared a moment later. "Hi," Skye said. Then she added brightly, "What now?"

Buyu slipped his pack off. "That's obvious. We eat."

———

It was a suggestion that appealed to everyone. They dropped into an aisle to make it harder for security cameras to pick them up. Then they ate a quick meal of ready bars, while crouched against the cargo containers.

As usual, Devi was full of ideas. "I've been thinking. We planned to stay in the elevator all the way to the end of the cable, but what if we're seen by a camera? We'll be safer if we go outside."

Skye glanced at Zia, then at Buyu. They both looked as confused as she felt.

"Outside?" Buyu asked. "We're not halfway to the top yet."

"Sooth. But we can ride up on the outside of the elevator car as easily as we can on the inside. There might be cameras outside, but nobody's going to check them." He looked around expectantly, but no one said a word. Devi frowned. "What's wrong? We've all got skin suits." He tapped his backpack. "We've all got nutrient packs to keep our suits supplied."

"Devi," Zia said, "it's two days to the top."

"So? We brought enough nutrients to last twice that long. It's a good move. Really. No one will ever check the cameras out there."

"I don't get it," Buyu said. "How are we supposed to get outside? I mean, if we open an airlock, an alarm could sound."

"I brought a bubble recipe."

"A what?" Skye asked.

"A bubble recipe. I fabricated it, using information from city library." Devi burrowed in his pack. Then he pulled out a small canister no bigger than his hand. "This is it. Inside this canister is a team of Makers. They're dormant now, but when they're sprayed on an inert mass, they'll work together to reengineer its molecular structure."

"Inert" meant that Devi's recipe wouldn't work on living things, but only on non-living objects—like the wall of the elevator car. It would rearrange the way atoms bonded to one another, but to produce what? "What's it supposed to do?" Skye asked.

Devi grinned. "It's a bubble recipe, Skye. We'll use it to manufacture a human-sized bubble in the elevator wall."

"A hole?" Zia asked. "That'll cause a decompression emergency—"

She stopped in mid-sentence, when Devi gave her a look that clearly said she was talking like an idiot.

"It's a movable bubble," Skye guessed. "It'll carry us from the inside of the elevator car to the outside, without ever creating an opening for air to escape."

"Exactly," Devi said, with a stern glance at Zia. "And of course it'll repair the wall behind us, so no one will ever know we were here."

"You planned this, didn't you?" Skye added. "You expected to go out early."

Devi shrugged. "This trip would be pretty pointless if we got caught sneaking around inside the elevator."

"I guess so." She looked at Zia and laughed at the tense expression on her face. "Don't look so worried! This could be a lot like jumping. Only backwards, because the elevator is falling *away* from the planet. And besides, anything is better than cuddling with lydras."

There were no windows on the warehouse floor, so it was impossible to know how thick the outside walls might be. Devi looked a little worried as he stood on a stack of containers at the end of an aisle, examining a featureless wall. Then he shrugged. "Oh well. The bubble won't form if the wall is too thin."

Oh well? Skye did not feel that casual.

"How do we even know this is an outside wall?" Zia demanded. "What if there's a room on the other side?"

Devi glanced down the length of the warehouse. "This has got to be a full-size floor. Look at it. It's the width of the elevator car. Right Buyu?"

Buyu looked a little doubtful, but he shrugged. "Looks like it."

"This is an outside wall," Devi said firmly.

Skye kept quiet. He was probably right.

She hoped he was right.

"Don't blow it, Devi," Zia growled. "That bottle looks like it holds only enough for a single use."

"Sooth." Devi was sweating now; his taut cheeks gleamed. "Okay. Stand back. And, well, close your hoods just in case."

In case the recipe malfunctioned and punched a hole all the way through the wall. That would cause a decompression catastrophe, as the air on this floor rushed out into airless space.

Skye whispered to her suit to close the hood. Ord was sitting on her shoulder. She reached up to take a firm grip on one of its tentacles. Devi sealed his own hood. Then, without another word, he sprayed the recipe in a neat oval equal to his own height.

At first the wall only looked wet, but after several seconds it took on a bumpy texture. Then it started to stretch, sinking toward the middle, while erupting in a ridge all around the edge of the oval. "It's working," Devi said, his voice reaching Skye through the radio system. He waved at them. "Come over here. Come quickly."

They gathered close around him.

"Okay. Let's do it. Just push yourselves into the soft wall . . ." He touched the wall with his hand. Then he leaned against it. His shoulder sank into the lumpy matter.

Skye could not believe it. "Devi! This can't be right. What if the wall hardens around us?" Then they would be trapped inside its structure. "You said it was going to be a bubble."

Devi nodded, as he squeezed even deeper into the muck. "Sooth. It is a bubble. A bubble of softened matter. Come on. Push your way in. It's a molecular reaction, and it won't last forever."

"*Zeme dust*," Zia muttered, but she pressed in next to him. Skye could do nothing but follow. Ord was still on her shoulder. It wrapped a tentacle around the strap of her backpack and held on tight. Skye slipped an arm around Devi's waist. As she did, her hand slid into the disturbed matter of the wall. It felt like heavy, wet sand.

Buyu pressed in next to her. She held him with her other arm. She was facing Zia. They stared at each other as the melting wall oozed over them, sliding across their shoulders, around their legs, over their visors . . .

After a few seconds, Skye could no longer see Zia's terrified eyes.

She knew they were completely covered when she felt a pressure against the arm that encircled Buyu's waist. Something on that side pressed against them. She imagined the wall hardening, returning to its former structure. Meanwhile, more goop flowed slowly past. It was like standing in a river of mud. She felt half crushed, squashed up against Devi while Buyu leaned against her. "I can hardly breathe," she whispered.

"It won't be long," Devi said. His voice sounded strained. A moment later, he vanished.

He dropped out of Skye's encircling arm as if a giant had yanked him away. "Devi!" She thought she heard him swear.

Then Zia was screaming. "*I'm falling! I'm falling!*" It was a cry of utter terror, like nothing Skye had ever heard before.

"Zia!"

"I've got her," Devi shouted. Skye could hear his harsh breathing. "Skye, reach down. Give me a hand."

"Where?"

She felt Buyu's grip tighten on her waist. "Get ready to slap the outside wall with your hot zones," he warned.

The softened wall abruptly gave way. Skye popped out into a sideways world, defined by the vast, lightless wall of the elevator car. She felt herself slip. The pull of Deception Well was far less than what it had been in Silk, but it was still real. Buyu caught her arm, slowing her fall. She twisted hard, and slapped her other hand against the wall of the elevator car. The hot zone of her glove bonded. A second later her boots connected. "Secure!" she shouted.

Buyu dropped her hand and swung sideways out of the closing bubble. His skin suit bonded at his shins and gloves, leaving him safely crouched against the vertical wall.

Only then did Skye look down.

They had emerged from the elevator car less than two meters above its base. Devi hung upside down, bonded to the wall by the hot zones on his shins. Zia dangled from his outstretched arms, with sixteen thousand kilometers of empty space beneath her. She didn't move. She didn't say a word. Skye wondered if she had fainted. Far beyond her, Deception Well had shrunk to a dark sphere only a little bigger than a soccer ball held at arm's length.

"*Help me,*" Devi whispered, his voice trembling. "I can't pull her up from this position."

"Oh, Zia." Skye spoke to her suit DI, "I'm climbing." The hot zones released their grip on the wall, one hand or one foot at a time so that she was able to scramble down the two meters to the bottom of the elevator car. Buyu climbed down on Devi's other side. There was an awkward moment as they tried to decide how to hold on to the wall and reach for Zia. After a second, Skye decided it was a matter of hanging on sideways. Buyu agreed. When they were both locked in place, they leaned together over the edge.

They each took one of Zia's arms.

It was too dark to see Zia's eyes through the arc of her visor, but her voice whispered over the radio. "*Don't drop me.*"

"Never, ado," Skye swore. "Not in a million years."

"On two," Devi said. "One, two—"

They yanked Zia up. They pulled too hard, forgetting about the reduced gravity. Zia shot up. Skye almost lost her grip, but Zia managed to slap her gloves against the elevator wall before she could bounce away forever. She landed on top of Devi. For several seconds no one moved. Skye's hood filled with the sound of her own panicked breathing. Then Zia uttered a little cry. She crawled clear of Devi, her breath coming in wracking sobs. Then the transmission from her suit switched off.

Skye scrambled to her side. She put her arm around her. "Hey, we're okay now."

Zia's shoulders heaved. Her whole body trembled. Skye huddled close to her, whispering nonsense, "It's okay, Zia. Everything's okay."

After a few minutes, Zia calmed down. She switched her suit radio back on. When she spoke, her voice trembled. "Skye, I've never been so scared before."

Skye squeezed her shoulder. "Me neither."

Zia leaned away from the wall, to look down past her feet. Skye followed her gaze. Dawn light glowed on the rim of the planet, sixteen thousand kilometers below them.

Chapter 19

*I*t was, Skye decided, a lot like going nowhere.

They had climbed to the top of the elevator car, the hot zones on their suits bonding and releasing as they moved hand and foot, hand and foot. Low gravity made the ascent easy. As Skye climbed, she felt like a fly crawling up a wall.

Skye and Zia stayed close together . . . just in case one of them needed comfort on the way. Skye's belly still felt hollow with fear. She couldn't imagine how Zia was feeling. They climbed in silence, until suddenly Skye gasped, as a new worry hit her. Zia turned at the sound.

"What?"

"Ord," Skye squeaked. "Where's Ord?" She hadn't seen it since they spilled out of Devi's badly designed bubble.

Zia squinted through her visor. "It's on your shoulder."

Skye turned to look. She could just see a flash of gold out of the corner of her eye. She reached up to touch the little robot, to assure herself it was all right. She waited for a tentacle to wrap affectionately around her hand. But Ord did not stir. Through her gloved fingers, its body felt oddly stiff. Almost frozen.

Zia's frown deepened to a scowl. She poked at it, but still Ord did not move. "Is it dead?"

"Don't say that."

Devi climbed up on her other side. He touched Ord too, tugging at one of the long tentacles wrapped around Skye's pack strap. "It's sure not active. I guess it wasn't made to work in vacuum. You know, without our suits, we'd fail out here too."

"No kidding!" She felt the hot sting of tears in her eyes. Whenever she and Zia had jumped, she'd been careful to leave Ord behind, locked up somewhere. This time, though, she hadn't thought about its safety at all.

"Hey," Devi said gently. "All I meant was, it's probably gone dormant."

She blinked hard, searching for his eyes behind the shadowed curve of his visor. "You think so?"

"Well, why not? It doesn't look damaged. It just looks . . ."

"Cold," Zia suggested.

"Sooth. Cold."

Skye fingered one of Ord's tentacles. It was stiff, and harder than usual, but otherwise it looked normal. "I guess we'll find out when we reach the lifeboat."

They started climbing again. It was only a few minutes later when they reached the top. Buyu and Zia tramped away from the edge, but Skye could not resist the allure of the abyss. She rolled out on top of the elevator car. Then she sat up.

Her legs dangled over the side. Her gloved hands clenched the lip as she leaned forward, looking down, swinging her feet over . . . sixteen thousand kilometers of nothing.

Morning spilled over the horizon of the little world far, far below them. So very far, yet she could still feel the insistent presence of that world in the weak gravity that let her sit, instead of floating away. How could Deception Well reach out so far, through so much empty space, to affect her? Gravity. Invisible and ever present. This was surely the craziest moment of her life.

She leaned back, looking over her shoulder now at the elevator column. Kheth's light had not yet reached this far. It was still night here. They were in the planet's shadow, so the column looked like a vast, featureless, black wall. Skye squinted, but she could not make out the track the elevator followed. She could see no sign at all that they were moving.

For a moment she felt disoriented, wondering if the car had stopped.

Then she looked up. A few kilometers overhead, the black column blazed brilliant silver. Sunlight! Of course. The end of the elevator column would swing out of the planet's shadow first, catching the light long before sunrise chased away the night in the rainforest at the elevator's base.

The boundary of darkness and brilliant light raced toward them, banishing all her doubts about the elevator car's speed. They were shooting toward that silvery light. She held her breath, and within a handful of seconds they slid from starlit night to blinding day. Devi whooped.

Skye turned to look for him, and found him only a few steps away, standing on the edge of the car, his arms outstretched as if were ready to take the whole of that magnificent vista in his embrace.

She shared his exhilaration. Throwing back her head, she howled—a tiny spark of radio noise—the voice of life—in a vast and beautiful galaxy. When her lungs were empty, she refilled them again with a deep breath of manufactured air that tasted better than any air she had ever breathed before.

It didn't get boring after that.

Not exactly.

She felt a little discouraged, though, when Zia commented dryly, "You know Skye, we're going to be out here two days."

Two days.

An awfully long time in a skin suit.

Now that they were in full sunlight, Skye once again experienced the odd sensation that they were not moving. "Sooth," Devi said, when she mentioned it to him. "Moving at a constant speed is almost the same thing as standing still. If you're not speeding up or slowing down, if you're not turning, if there's no wind in your face, or landmarks sliding past, then there's no way to tell whether you're moving or not. It's not motion that the body senses. It's *change* in motion. Here on the elevator car, everything is constant, including our speed."

Sooth. Deception Well was so far away now that Skye could not perceive it getting smaller from moment to moment. Only when she looked again after several minutes did she notice a difference. The only possible reference was the elevator column itself, but their speed blurred any landmarks that might be there.

It was, she decided after a while, a lot like going nowhere.

—◊◊◊—

There might be no sensation of moving, but progress could be measured in other ways. The pull of gravity continued to decline the further they rose above the planet. Deception Well continued to shrink in size, until it seemed impossible that such a tiny sphere could anchor a structure as immense as the elevator column. Most embarrassing, Skye's bladder continued to swell, until the pressure became unbearable.

She switched off her suit radio. Then she closed her eyes and whispered to the DI, "*I have to pee.*" Her cheeks grew hot as she said it. She knew a skin suit could be used for days and days without a break so long as it was supplied with liquid nutrients. A skin suit was almost a living thing. It consumed the same liquid nutrient diet that she sucked from a feeding tube that would emerge by her mouth whenever she asked for it.

So obviously her skin suit must be able to handle the other end of the digestive cycle—but despite all the time Skye had spent jumping off the elevator column, and even during her trip to Deception Well, she had never investigated its humble functions.

Her suit DI did not answer for several seconds. Finally, it spoke in its soft, female voice, sounding puzzled. "Is this a query?"

"Yes," Skye said, her voice low, as if someone might hear her. "Is there some special procedure . . . something I'm . . . supposed to do . . . when I pee?"

"Urination requires the contraction of the smooth muscles surrounding the bladder. Do you require assistance with this?"

Skye covered her face with her hands. Her cheeks felt so hot she thought they might melt. "No! I just . . . I mean . . . I should just pee, right? And the skin suit will handle the . . . the waste?"

"That's correct. All bodily wastes are broken down and recycled into nutritional components."

"Okay then." She stared out at the abyss for several seconds. Then she gave in, feeling like a little kid who had waited too long.

To her surprise, there was no sensation of liquid flooding her legs. The suit absorbed it all, so that she experienced only a rush of intense warmth that remained steady as she emptied her bladder, then faded gradually when she was through.

Quite convenient, really.

Heat was a problem. They were far above any sheltering atmosphere. Kheth's light poured over them, undiluted by layers of air, or by a protective canopy like the one that covered Silk. The heat was intense, so after a while they climbed a few meters down the shady side of the elevator car. They moved again as the light advanced, so that they stayed always in shadow. As the hours passed, they eventually climbed all the way down the side of the car, then across the bottom, and up again on the other side.

"It's not just the light we can see that could hurt us," Devi said. "There's a lot of hard radiation up here. Our suits can screen out some of it, but most of our protection comes from the medical Makers in our bodies. They're always working hard to repair any damage to our cells."

"Cell damage is repairable . . . right?" Zia asked.

"Oh sure. So long as our nutrients hold out."

Just as dawn had touched the end of the elevator column first, so day lingered there the longest. Night flowed up from the planet, a sharply defined shadow that silently engulfed the elevator car. Skye turned, to watch the shadow-line climb beyond them, higher and higher along the column until, just before the last of the light disappeared, she was able to make out a silver parasol, gleaming in the distance.

"Devi, look!"

It was the counterweight at the end of the elevator column. The end of their journey was in sight! A cheer went up among their small group, but even before it died away the light failed. Then only the milky nebula could be seen, and a few bright stars.

———

Skye fell asleep bonded to the top of the elevator car. The pack got in her way, and every time she wanted to turn over, she awoke. She didn't sleep much.

Daylight came, and they began a second migration around the car, following the cool shadows, staying out of the light. Had Yulyssa realized yet that Skye was missing? Or would she assume Skye had decided to spend an extra night with Zia?

Ord still did not move.

Skye slept better the next night, though she awoke early. It was still dark on the elevator car. Blinking, she looked up.

Dawn light had drawn a silver crescent on the counterweight. Skye gasped, astonished at its size. It had not looked nearly so big last night. Now she watched the crescent of light widen to reveal an immense disk sitting atop arching struts that sprouted from the elevator column like branches, holding up a shimmering gray sky.

The counterweight balanced the mass of the elevator column. Without it, the column would collapse, plunging downward into the planet's gravity well, falling through the atmosphere and striking the world with such force that most of the life there would likely be destroyed.

The counterweight.

Skye continued to gaze at it as the elevator ferried them upward.

———

As they neared the end of their journey, the elevator car slowed. It slipped between the arching struts, each one as wide as the widest tower in Silk, but built on a curve so that its base rested on the column while its far end extended well out beneath the gray roof of the counterweight. What would it be like to climb one of those struts? To walk up its back until it was possible to touch that gigantic roof?

Skye smiled. Maybe someday she would try it.

Buyu stood gazing directly overhead. "I think we should get off the top of the car," he said quietly. "We don't want to be trapped against a roof."

Skye peered upward, to where the track dove into a black circle carved out of the counterweight. It had to be a shaft. Squinting, she made out flecks of white glowing within the dark circle. "That's starlight! Buyu? Do you see it? Those are stars peeping through an elevator shaft. We're going to be carried straight through to the other side of the counterweight."

So they stayed where they were—and it proved a good decision. Kheth's brilliant light vanished abruptly as the elevator car entered the shaft. Walls slipped past only a few centimeters away. Buyu's sigh was audible over the radio system. "Zeme dust. If we'd tried climbing down the side of the car, we would have been crushed."

The elevator carried them up past dimly lit loading bays, floor after floor of them, each filled with ingots of pure elements: metals, and carbons, and things Skye could not name, all formed into precise blocks each the size of a house, stored here against the day they would be needed in some construction project. Perhaps they would be used in the creation of the great ship. Perhaps they would bide here, awaiting some other future not yet foreseen.

"I had no idea the counterweight had so many levels," Zia said softly. "And we're only seeing a tiny part of it, aren't we? There's room here for a whole new city!"

"Several cities," Devi said, "if the ecology can be balanced."

Room for new people and new cultures, Skye thought. She looked up, to the patch of starry darkness looming overhead, thinking about the hidden lifeboats that had to be out there, somewhere.

The elevator moved slowly now, only a meter or so per second. Zia said, "Let's lie flat. We don't want to be seen."

Sooth.

They pressed themselves against the roof. Skye kept her head up just high enough to peer over the edge of the car. As they rose into the next loading bay, she glimpsed several figures in skin suits near the far wall, all of them waving cheerfully at the arriving car. Instantly, she ducked her head.

A few seconds later the roof of the car drew even with the roof of the loading bay, leaving them safely concealed within the shaft. Then at last it happened.

They stopped.

Skye sat up slowly, staring at the walls of the elevator shaft, hardly able to believe they were really here.

She craned her neck, looking up. The shaft extended for another ten meters or so. Then it ended. Starlight and the milky threads of the nebula filled the void.

Buyu chuckled. "We could jump from here."

"And never fall back down," Devi said dryly. "It's a lot safer to climb."

Skye wanted to tell them both to shut up. She worried: What if their radio traffic was picked up by the skin suits in the loading bay? That shouldn't happen. The skin suits used select frequencies, picking up only those transmissions coded for them . . . just like a phone call.

Still, she could not shake the sense that someone might "overhear" them. Did the personnel on the counterweight scan for all radio signals?

Why would they?

No one knows we're here, Skye reminded herself.

"Let's go," Devi said. "We don't have a lot of time to get ready for our crossing to the construction zoo."

Chapter 20

Reaching the construction zoo was a matter of timing . . . *and insanity,* Skye amended, when Devi pointed out the zoo in the distance. She squinted at the chain of lights, looking at them sideways, trying to force them into better focus. Her vision improved with remarkable speed—and abruptly Skye realized why. She spun on Devi. "The zoo is coming really fast, isn't it?"

"About as fast as you were falling at the end of your record setting jump," Devi said quietly. Then he added, "It's within the tolerance of the jump cables."

Zia groaned. "That jump almost broke me in half! Now you're telling me I have to do it again?"

"No," Skye said. "I'm the only one who needs to go."

"The two of us," Devi corrected. "You could have trouble getting the lifeboat open."

"Make it three," Buyu said. "There's a lot more to the zoo than your lifeboat, Skye. It could be dangerous."

Zia sighed. "Buyu's right. There could be lydras. So I'm going too—but *zeme dust!*—why is the zoo moving so fast?"

"It's not the zoo," Skye said. "It's us."

Devi grunted. "The elevator column turns with the planet. We go around once every day—whether we're at the top of the column or the bottom. Which means that everywhere except at PSO we're not in orbit. We're either going too fast, or we're going too slow. That's why, if we stepped away from the column, we would fall away—either toward the planet or away from it, depending on where we are."

Zia nodded slowly. "But the construction zoo *is* in orbit," she said tentatively. "So it goes around the planet at its own speed?"

"Right. And that's a different speed than ours. The zoo takes about two hours longer to make a full circle."

Buyu spoke thoughtfully. "So it's not really shooting towards us. Actually, we're catching up."

Devi nodded in agreement. "Though you can't tell by looking."

They were silent a moment, watching the approaching lights. Then Skye added softly, "If their periods are only two hours different in every day, then it'll be days before the elevator and the zoo pass one another again, won't it? Devi, you got us here just in time . . . and this is our only shot."

In the time they had been talking, the construction zoo had grown much larger. Now Skye could just make out circular sections of the great ship being assembled in the zoo, tiny white rings strung in a line, one after the other, their neat order disturbed here and there by softer shapes that she could not identify.

"This is it," Devi agreed somberly. "There's no way we can camp out here until the next transit. We have to cross now."

When Skye turned to look at him, she discovered him down on his knees on the wide plain of the counterweight. He was setting up a knee-high tripod that held the launch gun. She'd seen the gun before, when they were planning this expedition. It was a modified version of the festival guns used to launch dissolving streamers high in the air of Silk. Devi had boosted its power, and added a low-intensity laser beam for targeting. The harmless laser would strike an object and be reflected back to a sensor on the gun, giving them an exact measure of just how far away it was, and the relative speed of its approach. "The targeting system will track the zoo while calculating its distance, direction, and speed," Devi had explained. "Then it will launch our cable."

"Cord," Skye corrected. The cables used for jumping off the elevator column were called cords. The end of the cord would strike the target and bond to it, creating a seamless high-strength joint. Several seconds after that the slack would run out. By that time they would all be tied in. When the cord went taut they would be yanked off the counterweight together.

Of course a sudden, extreme change in speed could be deadly— running into a wall at a thousand meters per second was never a good idea—so the cord would stretch, just as it did on a jump, to cushion the shock. Hopefully, it would be enough.

With her palm raised, Skye turned to Zia. "I'm scared."

Zia slapped her open hand, completing the jump ritual: "And I'm your mother."

"Okay," Devi said, peering at a display on the back of the gun. "We've acquired the target."

"We have enough cord, right?" Zia asked nervously.

"Sooth. Just enough. The zoo will pass between four and five kilometers above us."

Skye looked at the approaching construction zoo. Now she could easily see the white rings that would someday be part of the great ship. Following after them, she made out a smaller, darker wheel, with lights all around its curved edge. That would be the workers' habitat. They would need to stay away from that.

Strung through the center of the nearest white rings was a long line of irregular blobs, like poorly-made beads on an invisible wire. They glinted different colors, from pure white, to rose, to red and blue and purple. There was even an empty space between two of them that Skye guessed to be a bead of purest black, made invisible by the black background of space and the harsh light of Kheth. "Those beads," she said softly. "They're construction material for the great ship, aren't they? Like the ingots we saw in the loading bays. They're made of different kinds of matter."

"Sooth," Devi said. "They look irregular because they've been partially used. There's a big cache of ingots halfway down the line of rings. That's where we'll find the lifeboat. Hey—look at the far end of that ingot chain."

Skye squinted as she looked at the last bead in the string. It was smaller than the rest, bright orange in color. And . . . *it moved!* She gasped when she saw it. The bead unfolded, blossoming into a flower whose petals were long, writhing tentacles, blazing orange in the light of the distant sun. "It's a lydra," she said in wonder.

"Sooth," Zia agreed. "A full-sized construction beast. It's getting construction material from the ingots." Then she added in a soft voice, "We'll need to stay away from the big lydras."

Skye couldn't decide just how big this one was, but it had to be far, far bigger than even the biggest monster in the shipping crate.

"There's something else we'll need to stay away from," Buyu said, his arm raised as he pointed at an object far beyond the line of the construction zoo.

It was only a dot in the distance, but when Skye squinted she could make out a flash of red and green lights. "It's a ship," she said. "Tannasen?"

"Sooth," Buyu agreed. "That's *Spindrift*, coming in to pick up supplies."

When Devi spoke, he sounded grim. "*Spindrift* is equipped with robotic arms. If Tannasen sees us, he could try to grab us."

"*Yuck*," Zia said. "That's not the kind of hug I've dreamed about. We have to stay out of sight, gang. As best we can."

Skye knelt by the gun, studying the display. Her skin suit flexed, then hardened, helping her hold the position in the microgravity environment. The zoo was only eighteen kilometers away, and rushing on them with frightening speed. She could see the gun turning on its mount as it tracked the first ring in the line. "We should tie into each other already," she said, slipping her pack off her shoulder. Her gloved hand brushed Ord's frozen tentacle. Ord had not moved or responded in any way since they'd gone outside the elevator car. She could almost feel the chill of its tissue—a stunning cold that settled around her heart.

She drew a deep breath to steady herself. *What we're doing . . .*

it's more important than anything else. This thought didn't make her feel better about Ord—it only made her more determined.

She reached into her pack and pulled out three pairs of cylindrical cassettes. Each pair was linked by a few millimeters of jump cord, with more cord spooled inside. "I'm going first," she announced.

Buyu, Devi, and Zia all started to protest, so Skye said it louder. "I'm going first! No argument, okay?"

Something in her voice must have convinced them she meant it, because this time no one said anything.

She handed one pair of cassettes to Devi, and one to Zia. Then, with the third in hand, she felt behind her back for the socket she had recently added to her suit. She found it, and a moment later the cassette snapped into place. "Got it!"

"Compatibility check in progress," her suit DI announced. "Ten, nine, eight . . ."

"I'm in too," Devi said as he locked a cassette into the back of his own suit. "I'm going second."

Skye felt a slight pressure on her back as Devi tugged at the dangling cassette, unspooling a meter of thin gold cord. He snapped its end into the jump socket on the belly of his suit. Now they were linked, back to front.

Zia tied in behind Devi. Buyu linked to Zia. When they were pulled off the counterweight, the cassettes would unreel hundreds of meters of jump cord, cushioning the shock of their leap across the void, and putting distance between them so they wouldn't crash into each other.

Skye looked up, to check on the progress of the construction zoo—and gasped. It was almost directly overhead. She glimpsed three huge lydras at work among the separate sections of the great ship.

Quickly, she turned back to the gun. The muzzle was pointing straight up. Grabbing the cord that dangled from a cassette on the gun, she inserted it into her belly socket.

"Compatibility check in progress," the suit DI said again. "Ten, nine, eight . . ."

The gun went off.

Skye could not hear it of course—there was no air to carry the sound—but she saw a flash of motion as the anchor shot away. Gold cord paid out behind it, glistening like a single thread of a spider's web. She knew it must be unreeling several meters every second, yet it looked perfectly still.

Her suit DI announced, "Compatibility check complete. Integration at one hundred percent."

The gun had picked as its target the first white ring in the construction zoo. Crouching on the counterweight, Skye watched the narrow section pass overhead.

In a tense voice Devi said, "Order your suits to release their bonds with the counterweight. Hurry! We can't be attached when the cord goes tight."

Sooth. Skye didn't want to think about what might happen if the suits were still bonded to the counterweight. Would the cord give way first? If so, the broken end could snap back with enough force to slice them to ribbons. If the suits broke, their bodies would probably tear apart along the same fracture lines.

"Deactivate all hot zones!" Skye ordered her suit DI.

The DI sounded puzzled. "Are you sure?"

"Yes! Yes." She touched the cassette. "Look. I'm tied in."

"That line is not secured—"

"I don't care!" Skye shouted. "Don't argue with me! Just deactivate all hot zones. *Now.* The line will be secured in just a few—"

The gun shattered. In the same instant, Skye felt a hard yank against her waist. The cord had gone taut! And the sudden tension had been enough to break the gun into three large pieces. Her eyes went wide as she watched the fragments spiral away into the void. Somewhere out there, the cord must have found a target . . . but she was still attached to the counterweight. "The line's secure!" she screamed at her suit DI. "Deactivate—"

She broke off in mid-sentence as she felt her boots peel free, from the heels to the toes. Before she quite knew what was happening, she was yanked off the counterweight. The force of it knocked the air out of her lungs. She hurtled upward, feeling like an abused dokey on the end of a giant's leash. A barely perceptible backward jerk let her know that Devi had launched behind her. Part of her was glad, but most of her was terrified. She watched the construction zoo pass overhead. She expected to find herself hurtling closer and closer . . .

But to her surprise, the zoo grew farther away. What was happening?

Think! she ordered herself. It was hard, when she could scarcely get a breath beneath the crushing pressure of this lift.

Still, she tried to wrap her mind around the problem. It was a way of keeping her terror under control. *Think.*

Getting yanked off the counterweight was like jumping off the column, except she had already been moving at top speed while she stood there waiting. On a jump, she would fall for a while before she hit the end of her cord, but today she was already at the cord's end in the moment she left the counterweight. So. If she could turn around, she would see the counterweight racing away.

There was no way she could turn around. A horrible pressure was crushing every cell in her body. She could not move, not even to twitch a finger.

But I'm alive! she thought defiantly. *I can still think.* So the cord must be stretching, as it was supposed to. Stretching to slow her down gradually, to absorb her momentum so she would not be smashed to jelly inside her suit—even if it felt that way.

It might have been a few seconds. It might have been minutes. She had no way of knowing. She was too scared to keep track of time. But at last the pressure eased. She gasped for breath and filled her lungs over and over again. She could hear somebody jabbering over the radio, but she could not make out the words. Her eyes were watering. She blinked several times and shook her head. Then she looked again.

The first white ring lay just ahead of her. It looked immense . . . bigger around than any building in Silk. She could make out an odd, circular grain in the white metal, so she knew it was close, maybe only a few hundred meters away. Strung through its center was the chain of colorful ingots she had seen before.

Only now it was easy to see that each "bead" of refined matter was the size of a small house.

The ingots and the great ring hung in the dark, unmoving. Not receding. Not approaching—which meant she was moving at the same speed as the construction zoo.

She put out a cautious hand and touched the cord. It was taut. She could feel it sliding into the cassette. So. She *was* moving, but slowly. Very slowly. It had to be that way. If the cord hauled her in too quickly, she would be slammed against the ring and crushed.

She reached behind her back, feeling for the link that tied her to Devi. She found it and tugged gently, twisting so that she could look over her shoulder.

Devi trailed behind her, a few hundred meters away. Zia drifted beyond him, and Buyu was a tiny figure at the end of the line. The cords that tied them all together were too thin to see, so they seemed to float unattached, just like the ingots of refined matter that were part of the zoo.

The zoo.

They were inside it. Immense rings that would become the hull of the great ship hung in a long line behind them. It was like looking down the body of a toy snake, the kind made of hoop-segments linked together by magnetic forces, except here the chain of ingots hung within the rings. Far down the line, Skye could see the cache of unused ingots. Devi had said it was midway along the line of rings. It looked like a fleet of tiny, colorful bubbles frozen in place, as if they'd been captured in glass. The lifeboat would be there, somewhere, though they were still too far away to see it. Beyond the cache, more rings stretched away into the dark distance.

Motion caught Skye's eye. Her gaze shifted back, to discover an immense lydra perched on the rim of the nearest ring. It looked like an orange sun, with tentacles that were great solar flares. As she watched, it reached out to a purple lydra riding on an ingot. They hooked tentacles, and slowly the purple one was drawn across the gap and onto the ring, leaving the ingot behind.

Skye looked again toward the distant end of the zoo. Beyond the last of the white rings, she could just make out the illuminated wheel of the workers' habitat. She squinted, looking for motion, for some sign that someone might be outside. Had they been discovered?

She saw no suited workers. The only movement came from the lydras, and from the faraway flash of *Spindrift's* red and green lights.

Suddenly, Skye was aware of someone talking to her. She shook her head again, and looked around.

"*Skye,*" Zia was saying. "Skye, answer me. Skye! Are you okay?"

"Oh, I, uh, *sooth,*" she stuttered, flushing in embarrassment. How many times had Zia called her name? "I'm okay. Zia, how about you?"

"Battered but breathing," Zia answered.

"Me too," Devi said.

Buyu did not sound quite so confident. "My suit DI says I'll live," he groaned. "I'm not so sure."

Skye looked again at the ring ahead of them. It was a lot closer. Several more rings lay beyond it. She frowned. "I thought we were anchored to the first ring."

"We are," Devi said.

"Then the cord—"

"Is passing around all those other rings ahead of us."

Skye felt a new sweat break out across her sticky skin.

Zia, too, must have understood what might have happened, because she voiced Skye's concerns exactly: "We could have collided with any one of these rings."

Devi said, "The DI adjusted the length of the cord so that wouldn't happen."

"You've got a lot of faith in DIs," Buyu told him.

Devi chuckled drily. "Everything we're doing out here is coordinated by DIs. We don't have any choice but to trust them."

Skye kept her gaze fixed on the slowly approaching ring. "It could take hours for the cord to wind all the way in. We can't wait that long. And besides the ingot cache is in the other direction. So I say we anchor on the first ring we touch."

"Sooth," Devi said. "Let's do it."

So Skye spoke to her suit DI, giving it careful instructions as the ring loomed in front of her. The ring was a circular rib of smart steel, bright white, part of the structural skeleton of the great ship that would someday take shape here. Hundreds of small lydras crawled on its surface. Wherever they passed, there appeared shimmering patches of newly laid matter. Day by day, the ring of smart steel grew thicker.

Skye spread her arms, preparing for impact. She hoped she would wind up embracing steel, not lydra. She was close enough that she could see the cord bending down and around the ring. It had sliced through a green lydra, cutting off two of the creature's tentacles. Skye saw them adrift, not far away. She shivered. Blue fluid had frozen in massive crystal patches at the site of the wounds.

The ring grew closer. It was *huge*—big enough to encircle several elevator cars. Big enough to encircle the tower Devi had lived in. It was the size of a great ship.

The last few seconds blurred together as Skye plunged toward impact. The cord bent around the ring, but she was set to slam against its face. She braced herself. Then, just before she hit, a stranger's voice spoke over her suit radio. "Skye Object 3270a! How in the name of wonder did you get out here?"

Chapter 21

*B*efore Skye could figure out who was speaking or what to say, she slammed against the ring of white steel. "*Oof!*" Her breath whistled out of her lungs again, but the hot zones on her gloves and on her shins knit to the steel, securing her in place. At the same time her cassette stopped reeling in cord. "I'm set!" she whispered, as soon as she could get a breath. A small lydra squirmed only a hand-span away from her face. "Devi, who...?"

She turned around to look for the source of the voice, but she saw Devi instead, only a few meters away and coming in fast. She reached out to catch his arm but missed. He slammed against her. A moment later his hot zones had knit, nailing them both to the ring.

"And Divine Hand," the unknown voice said. "You need to work on your zero gravity technique."

"Tannasen," Devi panted. "I know his voice. He must have gotten our IDs from our skin suits."

This brought a good-humored chuckle from Tannasen. "Devi. Quick as ever, I see."

Skye's eyes went wide. The suit transmissions should be coded for privacy. "How can he hear us?" she blurted.

Tannasen answered that. "I've overridden your privacy option. City authority was a bit surprised when I reported your presence here."

Devi reached out to catch Zia before she hit the ring. "We're out of time, ados," Zia whispered as her gloves bonded. "Where's the lifeboat anyway?"

"Shh!" Skye didn't want Tannasen to know what they were after. She had hoped they would have a few hours to work their way back to the ingot cache and find the lifeboat. Now it seemed they would have only minutes. She craned her neck, looking for *Spindrift*, but the ship had disappeared behind the rings.

Buyu made his landing next. He caught himself on hands and feet, far more gracefully than the rest of them. Here in freefall his bulk didn't matter so much. "I saw it," he said.

The lifeboat? Skye scrambled to his side. "You did? Where?"

Tannasen was speaking at the same time, sounding a bit distracted, as if he were talking to someone else. "*What was that? Say again? . . . why wasn't I informed?*"

Buyu gestured back the way they had come. "Near the center of the ingot cache. I saw it eclipse a reddish nodule."

"You're sure you didn't see a carbon ingot?" Devi asked. "Some of them are black, just like the lifeboat."

"Sure I'm sure," Buyu answered, sounding insulted. "The object I saw was smooth. It had the right shape, and it was a lot smaller than the ingots."

"*. . . and maybe you should have listened to them!*" Tannasen snapped. After a moment he snorted. "Policy!" Then, in a dispirited voice he added, "Sooth. It sounds like they're after the lifeboat. I'll let them know. Yes. I'll bring them in."

Skye met Devi's gaze. She could just see his eyes through the curve of his visor. They glinted with determination. Looking down, she grasped the cassette at her waist. She didn't need it anymore. So she set it to rewind, then she let it go. It went speeding off into the void, winding up the extra cord. Let the lydras find it! Let them transform it into the bones of the great ship.

"We jump from one ring to the next," she said softly. She slapped the second cassette at her back. "We're still tied together, so if anyone misses, we can reel them in."

"Skye Object," Tannasen said. "Devi." He hesitated, as if he were checking a list. "Buyu Mkolu, and uh, Zia . . . Adovna. Listen to me. City authority thinks you're after the lifeboat. True?"

No one answered. Skye held her hands up to the others, gesturing at them to *wait*. Then she crouched against the ring. Taking careful aim at the next ring in the line, she launched herself across the gap.

"Skye—!" Tannasen barked. "Skye Object, listen to me. The lifeboat isn't here. It's been moved to a different orbit."

"What?" she cried. She couldn't believe it.

"It's what they're telling me," Tannasen insisted.

She was halfway across the gap between the two rings, and suddenly she felt helpless, unable to turn or change direction. If the lifeboat wasn't there, then everything they had gone through was for nothing.

Buyu spoke, in a low, dangerous voice she had never heard before. "City authority is lying. I saw the lifeboat in the cache."

Of course.

Skye stared down the tunnel of rings. She could see the colorful ingots of the central cache, fixed in place like frozen bubbles, but she could not see *Spindrift*. Where was the ship now? She hadn't glimpsed it for several minutes.

"*I* don't see the lifeboat," Tannasen said.

Devi answered, "It's hard to see."

"Sooth." Now Tannasen sounded truly puzzled. "What's going on? Why are you all out here?"

That was easy to answer. "Because I'm not the only one," Skye growled. Anger had replaced her sense of helplessness. City authority was *lying*. Were they so afraid of something new? "There are other lifeboats out there, Tannasen. And I think I know how to contact them."

The next ring was coming up fast . . . and abruptly Skye realized she was going to miss it. Instead of hitting its rim, she would pass right through its open center . . . and maybe through the centers of the next two rings.

She grinned. Which only meant she would get to the ingot cache sooner.

She felt the cord tug against her back as it stretched, slowing her down. "No!" she shouted. She reached back and yanked on it, hard. "Don't stop me." Her protest drowned out whatever Tannasen was saying.

"Skye . . . ?" Devi asked uncertainly.

"Are you slowing me down?" she demanded.

"Sooth, I—"

"Don't. I'm going to shoot all the way through to the ingot cache."

He hesitated a second, then, "Okay. You're on a good line for it. Better than me. I'll try not to drag."

She smiled. Devi knew what counted.

Tannasen was saying something, but she wasn't listening. Her attention had been stolen by the architecture around her. She swept through the ring, just missing its inside rim. Far overhead, a rust-colored lydra was unwrapping itself from an ingot in the long chain that passed through the ring's center. As she watched, its tentacles convulsed. It popped off the ingot, shooting straight for her. "Skye, look out!" Devi shouted.

"I see it!" She cringed, but already her motion had carried her past the lydra . . . while Devi was shooting straight toward it.

Skye reached back and grabbed the cord, twisting around so she could see him. *Zeme dust.* Devi and the lydra were about to collide.

She did the only thing she could. She put both hands on the cord and pulled *hard.* The jerk slowed her forward momentum while Devi sped up. The lydra's tentacles brushed his shoulders as he slipped past. "Devi! Are you—"

"I'm fine!"

Oh no.

Skye's eyes widened as she watched the lydra hit the segment of cord behind Devi, the one that linked him to Zia. Its tentacles wrapped around the thin line, one of them following it forward toward Devi, and another snaking back toward Zia. "Pop the cord off!" Skye screamed. "Now! Zia!"

Devi's end of the cord snapped free. He came speeding toward her as she swept through the next ring—but what had happened to Zia? Skye couldn't see her. She had disappeared behind the lydra's bulk.

"Zia!"

"Skye, I'm going to hit it! Buyu, pull me back. Quick!"

Buyu had just reached the second ring. Skye watched him kick the inside rim with both feet. His boots bonded and he yanked to a stop with his fists curled around the line. At least Skye assumed he held onto the line. She was too far away to see it, so it looked like he was performing a pantomime as he yanked back hard.

Zia popped into sight, so far away now she looked like a doll as she rose above the lydra. "Ha!" she shouted. "You missed me, you overgrown nightmare."

Sooth. The lydra was falling away from Zia, but now Zia and Buyu were far behind.

"That lydra was aimed at us!" Devi shouted. He sounded furious. "They were using it to stop us!"

"What? Who?" Skye looked around at him. He had almost caught up with her. In a few seconds he would glide past her, only three meters away.

"City authority," he said grimly. "It wasn't chance that sent that lydra jumping after us. Someone guided it. They wanted to snap the cord, separate us."

Guided it? Were lydras guidable? *Sooth.* They had to be. How else could they do the construction work? No wonder she had seen no human workers in the zoo. The engineers were cozy inside their habitat, guiding lydras through remote control.

She glanced over her shoulder. The ingot cache was only a few hundred meters away. From a distance, the ingots had looked like colorful bubbles caught in glass. This close, they looked like little planets, the kind in fantasy stories, where it was possible to walk all the way around the world in only a few seconds.

Motion drew her gaze overhead, in time to see another lydra pop off the ingot train. It shot toward them. "*Zeme dust*. Devi look." She pointed. "Another one."

This one was small, hardly a meter across. As it plunged toward them the glands of its underbelly could be seen shimmering in the crosshatch of light and shadow. Skye writhed to get out of the way, but instead of landing on her shoulders, the lydra dropped onto the cord. It clung there for only a second—slicing through the cord? Dissolving it? Whatever it did, the cord snapped. The lydra fell away. And Devi slipped past her, through the last ring and into the 3-D maze of the ingot cache.

In the shadow of an orange ingot, she could just make out the silhouette of a human figure waiting to meet him.

Chapter 22

*D*evi!"

"I see h—"

Devi's transmission was cut off as a new voice interrupted, speaking in a harsh, masculine timbre. This was definitely not Tannasen. "I don't know how you kids made it up here, but it's dangerous. More dangerous than you know. Come in to the habitat. We'll talk things over . . . and arrange your transport home."

Skye couldn't tell if it was the figure in the shadows speaking, but now that person stirred, moving into the light, revealing himself to be a man, tall and slender, in an orange skin suit. He straddled a sled. Its cylindrical surface was covered with tiny nozzles. Working in concert, the little jets could send him in any direction. Now he was moving to intercept Devi.

Devi was less than two meters away from a blue ingot the size of large room. If he could reach it, he could kick off, and dodge his pursuer. But he wasn't going to reach it. His trajectory would take him past it. Devi had no sled and the cord was broken, so there was no way he could stop, change direction, or run away . . . unless someone gave him a nudge.

Quickly, Skye wriggled out of her backpack, working the straps past Ord's frozen tentacles. With a pang, she wondered if Ord was still alive. And if it was, how long could it survive in vacuum? There was nothing she could do to help it now.

She got the backpack off just as she passed through the last great ring. Then she unplugged the nutrient line. Now she would have only a few hours before the suit used up its energy reserves. Given the circumstances though, that would be more than enough time to succeed . . . or to fail.

Holding the pack by a strap, she took careful aim. Then she slung it at Devi. "Heads up!" she shouted.

It almost missed.

But Devi had been alerted by her warning. He saw the pack and grasped at it, catching it on his fingertips. It was only a nudge, but it pulled him around, changing his trajectory so that now he angled across the face of the ingot, drawing gradually closer. He waited three seconds, four, then five. The man on the sled sped toward him, gesturing frantically, shouting something that Skye could not understand because she was shouting too. "Hurry Devi! Jump now! Go, go, go!"

He kicked out hard. Both feet hit the wall of the blue ingot, and he shot away, past the man on the sled. Skye smiled. His new trajectory was aimed to intercept her own path. "Catch my hands," he shouted. "Push off me, toward the red ingot. You have to get to the lifeboat, Skye. You're the only one who matters."

"No!" the man cried. "Don't you understand? You're destabiliz-ing—"

"Now!" Devi shouted. They caught each other's hands. For a moment she could look into his eyes. She could see the pride there. The determination. Then he pushed her away as hard as he could. Skye shot off, turning slowly as she went. The red ingot swung into sight. From the corner of her eye she could see the man on the sled racing toward her, but he was too far away to catch her. The red ingot loomed close. She kicked at it with one foot, launching herself deeper into the cache.

Ingots were all around her now, like huge boulders, glistening in a rainbow of colors. She dived from one to the next, kicking off hard every time. Buyu had seen the lifeboat near the center of the cache. As she careened from ingot to ingot she looked for it. *There.* A pure black egg-shape decorated with a few golden tatters left from its shattered solar sail.

"Devi, I see it!"

"Skye wait!"

She didn't listen. She kicked off one last ingot, launching herself at the lifeboat.

She was going fast, and she hit it hard. The impact set the lifeboat wobbling. She felt a fierce heat blaze in her gloves—but they weren't bonding! Somehow the hull had rejected the bond with her gloves. Now she slid helplessly across the rounded prow. "Bond!" she screamed at the DI. "Meld with the hull. *Now!*"

The DI answered in its calm female voice, "This surface will not accept a molecular link."

Zeme dust!

As she slid across the glossy black hull she tried to slow herself by friction alone. It was like trying to get a grip on polished ice. At the same time Devi was screaming at her to "*Kick off! Get out of the ingot cache!*"

No way.

She slid the length of the lifeboat. She was about to slip over the side when her fingers found a seam. She thrust her hands into it. It was like plunging them into a hard gel. She held on tight. Her legs swung around and she almost lost her grip. Almost, but not quite.

For a moment she didn't move. She could feel the lifeboat rocking under her belly. She could hear Devi shouting in her ear, his words mixed up with the frantic voice of the stranger so she couldn't understand either of them. Motion drew her eye. She turned, to see an ingot wobbling slowly past.

Her eyes widened in shock. When she had entered the cache, all the ingots had been motionless relative to one another. Had the man on the sled launched one after her? Did he want to kill her?

She twisted around, suddenly sure he would be right behind her. But what she saw was worse. Dozens of ingots were wobbling, drifting, colliding with each other and then bouncing away again . . . like slow motion billiard balls in a zero gravity box.

And if each ingot was a billiard ball, then Skye was the size of a soft and very crushable fly. What had the man on the sled tried to tell them?

Don't you understand? You're destabilizing—

Skye thought she could finish the sentence now: *You're destabilizing the ingots.*

The ingots were massive, but every time she had launched off one, she had given it a little bit of momentum—for every action there is an equal and opposite reaction. It was a classic rule of physics. Every ingot she and Devi kicked must have wobbled off its course, and now the slow, chaotic motion was spreading across the cache. The man on the sled hadn't been trying to stop them from reaching the lifeboat. He'd been trying to protect them by protecting the quiet order of the cache.

"Skye?"

"Devi, I didn't think—"

"Neither did I. Can you see a path out of the cache?"

She hesitated. "Devi, I can't leave now. I'm at the lifeboat."

"I don't care."

Tannasen's voice backed him up. "Devi's right, Skye Object. Curb your curiosity. It's not worth getting crushed."

A new worry touched her. "Devi, where are you? Are you safe?"

"I'm with Tannasen. In *Spindrift*." He sounded embarrassed. "He grabbed me with the ship's robot arms. Zia and Buyu are here too."

At least they were safe. But just how far could those robot arms reach? Could they pluck her out of the middle of the cache? She looked overhead, then underfoot, but she did not see the little research ship. The man on the sled had disappeared too, but then he would be crazy to follow her into this gyrating field. Just to be sure, she looked over her shoulder—and gasped.

A huge black ingot was wobbling only a few meters away. Was

it moving toward her? She watched it closely for several seconds before she was sure. *Sooth*. It was drifting slowly toward the lifeboat. Inevitably, it must collide.

And then what? Would the boat be damaged? Would its stubborn DI assume it was again under attack? Skye had to make contact with the DI before that happened—but to do that she had to get the lifeboat open.

Frantically she ran her fingers along the hidden seam. She felt for buttons, touchpads, levers. "Open," she whispered softly. "Open, open, open . . ." Not listening to Devi and Tannasen's frightened pleas.

Something gave way beneath her probing fingers. The seam widened. A neat section of the egg-shaped lifeboat lifted away on a hinge, revealing the white gleam of a gel membrane. Skye took one last glance at the mammoth ingot wobbling toward her on a slow collision course. Then she dove inside.

Chapter 23

There was no light at all inside the lifeboat. Skye skidded through the dark, bumping up against a smooth, curved something. A wall? She could feel it rocking slowly, echoing the wobble of the lifeboat.

"Hey," she whispered to her suit DI. "Make my suit glow, the way it did in the lava tube."

Even before she finished speaking, her suit began to give off a soft light. It revealed a narrow tentacle, sliding slowly down her right arm. *A lydra?* She yelped and brushed at it frantically. Then froze, as she realized what it must be.

"Ord?" she whispered. She turned her head, to find Ord perched on her shoulder, wide awake and mouthing words that she could not hear. "Ord!" Then to her suit DI she said, "Is there air here? Is it breathable?" From her research she knew the life support system was supposed to be working.

The DI assured her that indeed, it was quite safe to unfurl her hood. She did. Ord's little head turned to peer at her. Its tiny face wrinkled in a look of distaste. "Skye," it said primly. "You smell dirty."

She laughed. If that was the worst thing that could be said about her, she could live with it. "Let's just hope the lifeboat's DI can smell me too!"

She looked around. The interior of the lifeboat was much smaller than she had expected. It was shaped like an oblong capsule, its walls smooth and rounded and featureless except for four air vents. There was barely enough room for her to stretch full length. Of course, this chamber had been designed to hold only an unconscious baby. Truly, it was lucky she could fit inside at all.

She thought back to Tannasen's reports, and remembered that this space had been filled with a nutrient gel when he had found her.

Now it held only a pleasant atmosphere.

She eyed the air vents. They were covered with mesh screens, and each gap in the mesh pumped open and closed like mechanical lips—an army of lips breathing cool air into the chamber on one side and sucking it out on the other. Skye wondered why the vents were working. Why had the DI kept this chamber habitable for so many years? Was Devi right? Was it waiting for her to return?

Ord tapped her cheek. "Smart Skye. This is a nice, safe place to be."

Skye wasn't so sure. She thought of the mammoth ingot, drifting slowly toward the lifeboat. How long before it hit? Minutes, at most. What to do? What to do? The empty chamber offered no inspiration. All the lifeboat's control systems must lie hidden behind the walls.

Was Devi right? Was there anything left of the DI that had once existed here?

Her throat felt dry with worry, so she took a sip of nutrient juice from the straw inside her skin suit. When she looked up again, the chamber walls were aglow with a warm white light. A voice spoke. It sounded neither male nor female, but something in between. It said a word in a language she did not understand. At the same time, a section of the wall softened, stretching into a tall human shape. A moment later a man in a skin suit popped through the gel membrane. Skye recoiled.

This wasn't Devi and it wasn't the man on the sled. She knew it, because his skin suit was sparkling white. The stranger's head turned comically back and forth as he looked around the chamber. Then his hood unfurled to reveal a narrow, chiseled face, its harsh features capped by a stubble of closely-shaved hair. "You've got it working!" he exclaimed. "Skye Object, how did you do that?"

Skye shrank against the wall. "Tannasen?" she guessed.

"Sooth. We've met before." He winked. "Though I don't think you would remember." Then he added, as if it were an afterthought. "You've grown."

"Where's Devi?"

Tannasen hooked a thumb over his shoulder. "On *Spindrift*. Outside the ingot cache. We've got to get you out of here too." Then he shook his head. "I can't believe you've got this boat working. I know people who have spent years trying to get some response from this DI."

"It spoke to me."

His face got very still.

"It said something," Skye insisted. "I didn't understand the language."

"Can you repeat it?"

"I . . ." She shook her head. She could not.

Then an idea came to her. She turned to Ord, plucking it off a wall. "Ord, did you hear what the DI said? Do you remember it?"

"Yes, good Skye." Then Ord mimicked exactly the word they had heard. In a tone that sounded almost smug it added, "City library translates this as 'cargo child'."

"You understood it? Why didn't you say so?"

At the same time, Tannasen was musing, "Cargo child. Then it does recognize you . . ."

"So Devi was right!"

"Sooth. So far."

"I can't talk to it," Skye said. I don't know its language."

"Not surprising, considering how many languages we humans use. Well, if your little pet can translate, perhaps this DI can translate too? Ask it. Why not?"

Why not indeed? Skye swallowed hard. Then, gazing at the blank walls, she said, "Sooth. I am the cargo child. I've come back. Can you understand this language I'm using? Can you speak it?"

The man/woman voice responded immediately. "Yes, cargo child. We have waited for your return. Is the danger past?"

"The . . . danger?"

"We sought refuge in this system, but we were attacked—"

"That . . . was an accident," Skye whispered. "There is a nebula surrounding this system, full of stony pebbles, and tiny gnomes that feed on the solid matter . . ."

"Is the danger past?" it repeated.

She smiled weakly. This was the message she had come to deliver. "Yes." Then she said it louder. "Yes. The danger is past. We are safe, and it's time for the other cargo children to come home."

The DI did not reply. For a moment Skye wondered if it had stopped working again. Then Tannasen's hands flew up to cover his ears as a shriek roared out of his suit radio. He must have set his system to pick up any signals in the area. "By the Unknown God!" he shouted. "What is that?"

Skye laughed. "It's an all-clear, Tannasen! It's the signal the other lifeboats have been waiting for all these years. I always knew I wasn't alone."

The lights went out. The air vents whispered into silence.

In the darkness, Skye's skin suit glowed blue. She looked around in confusion. "Hello? Is something . . . wrong?"

The DI didn't answer.

"It's gone," Tannasen said softly.

"What?"

"It's been sitting here for twelve years without replenishing its energy supply. It must have used all the power it had left to send that signal."

She wrestled with a sudden sense of loss. "I . . . thought it could tell me who . . . who I am. Where I came from. Who my parents were . . ."

Tannasen drifted close. He put an arm around her. "You're Skye Object," he said gently. A warm smile unfolded on his face. "And as for the rest of your questions, young lady—they'll be answered when we pick up the next lifeboat."

"Then you really think—"

Suddenly the lifeboat shook. The chamber wall slammed up against them.

"The ingot!" Skye cried, as they bounced back and forth across the little chamber. "It must have hit us."

"Sooth. Let's get out of here while we still can."

Skye grabbed Ord. "Hold on tight, now," she warned it. "We're going outside again." Then she pulled on her hood. Tannasen had already wriggled out through the gel membrane. Skye followed him. It was a tight squeeze. The hatch that covered the membrane had been partly crushed in the collision. She fervently hoped no other ingot was heading their way.

At last she wriggled free, only to find herself sliding away across the lifeboat's slick hull.

"Whoa!" Tannasen called. "Wait for me."

As if Skye could stop.

He dove after her, and they linked hands. Skye took a quick look around. On one side the ingot cache looked like a field of nervous boulders, jostling in slow motion. "We don't want to go in there," Tannasen said.

"Sooth." On the other side, the ingots were nearly still. "That way then?" She pointed with her free hand.

"Naw." He jerked his thumb up past his face. "That way will be faster."

She looked overhead, to see *Spindrift* waiting, a short jump away.

It took them only a few minutes to get aboard. Ord revived again as soon as it hit air, while Skye dove straight into Devi's arms for a hug that soon included Zia, and Buyu too.

"Did you hear it?" Skye said. "The lifeboat sent a signal! Devi, you were right."

He shrugged. "I don't know, Skye. It might have been an all-clear, but . . . there haven't been any answering signals. Not one. We've been listening."

"Oh." Black disappointment washed over her. She didn't know what to say. She turned to look for Tannasen.

He was speaking to the ship, discussing the best way back to the end of the elevator column. After a moment, he looked up at their little group. "There are a lot of people in Silk who are happy to know you kids are still alive."

"It didn't work," Skye told him. "No other lifeboats have responded."

"Not yet, anyway." Tannasen's eyes glinted in good humor. "What's the speed of light?"

"What?"

"The speed of light. Basic knowledge."

Devi said, "Three hundred thousand kilometers per second."

"Give a sterling report to my favorite student! That's how fast a radio signal travels. Now answer this: How far is the outer edge of the nebula?"

Devi looked at Skye, giving her a chance to answer. She shrugged. "A long way. It takes . . . two hours? No, two and half hours for Kheth's light to travel that far. I remember hearing that somewhere."

"Absolutely right. So if a lifeboat is as far as the outer edge of the nebula . . . ?"

"Then it will take two and half hours just to receive the all-clear," she mused. "And another two and half hours before we hear its response—"

A strangely familiar, whistling note erupted in *Spindrift*'s main cabin. Listening to it, Skye felt a shiver run down her spine. "Hey. That sounds like—"

"The lifeboat's signal!" Zia finished for her. "Is it an answer?"

"It has to be," Buyu said. "And a lot sooner than five hours. Ados, we did it!"

Tannasen's brows rose, as his face broke into a grin. "Well of course five hours was only an estimate," he said. "A lifeboat that was closer wouldn't take nearly so long to respond."

—— ·~~· ——

Each waking lifeboat sent out its own all-clear signal, relaying the message across a vast swath of space surrounding the star called Kheth. Some of the lifeboats were years of travel time away, trapped in long, lonely orbits that would loop around Kheth only once in many centuries—if they were left undisturbed.

That wouldn't happen now. City authority could no longer deny the lifeboats existed. Solar sails were blooming throughout the nebula—and being shredded almost as quickly, though this time their DIs had been warned that this was a natural hazard, and not an attack.

The people of Silk saw the golden glints in the night sky and demanded that every lifeboat be gathered in. The loudest voices belonged to the oldest real people like Yulyssa, who had long ago faced the violence of the Chenzeme and survived. They were the first to say what everyone knew in their hearts to be true: *In a dangerous universe, it's our duty to help one another survive.*

Epilogue

*E*arly one evening, not long after their return to Silk, Skye and Zia arrived at the rooftop apartment of Siva Hand. City lights gleamed below them as they walked through the garden and up the stairs to Devi's rooftop observatory.

Devi sat on the railing, silhouetted against the milky wash of the nebula. His telescope loomed beside him, while Buyu stood on his other side, leaning against the rail.

"So we're all together again," Zia chirped. "How shall we get in trouble this time?"

Skye hadn't seen much of anyone since she'd gotten back. There had been hearings to attend, and disciplinary meetings and the obligatory media interviews. In the end, the city council decided to forgive rather than punish. It was the politically popular thing to do.

Ord dropped off her shoulder as she traded a hug with Devi, and then a soft kiss. She felt a bit awkward. Maybe he did too. Maybe that explained the unfamiliar tension she felt in his arms and in the muscles of his back. Did his smile seem forced?

"Look through the telescope," he said softly.

"Why? Have you found another lifeboat?"

"Sooth. It's the farthest away yet."

She bent to peer through the eyepiece at a faint gold gleam, wondering how many years it would be before this "cargo child" was brought into Silk. Even the nearest lifeboats would take months to retrieve.

"Tannasen's going out after them," Devi announced. "He's leaving in a few days."

"So soon?"

Zia laughed. "On the way down the elevator, Tannasen told me that he hasn't spent more than ten consecutive days in the city since *Spindrift* was made."

Devi said, "He's offered me a berth."

Dead silence greeted this announcement. Skye turned slowly away from the telescope, almost afraid to breathe, afraid that something might break inside her. But to her surprise, nothing did.

Oh, it hurt—worse than hitting the end of a four kilometer cord—but underneath that she was . . . not exactly happy, but *pleased*. And proud. Devi had been wanting something like this all his life.

Skye smiled. It wasn't that hard to do. She took his hands in hers. "You've accepted?"

He could not quite meet her gaze. "Not yet."

"But you will?"

"I don't know. It's for two years."

"That's a long time," Buyu suggested.

Was it? Skye would be all of sixteen when he got back. That didn't sound so very old anymore. She squeezed Devi's hands. "I'm going to miss you."

He scowled. "I haven't said I'm going yet."

"Oh you're going," she told him. "I think you should."

"You do?"

She nodded. "I am going to miss you. You know that."

He looked at her suspiciously. "You're trying to get rid of me, aren't you?"

She thought it best not to answer that. "You'll have to write me letters—"

"Listen to you! You can't wait to see me gone."

"—and make lots of exciting discoveries—"

"Skye—"

"—and . . ." Her voice caught. "And things will be different when you get back. I'll be different. Older. Devi, I haven't been an ado for very long."

He looked down at their clasped hands. "Sooth. That's part of it too."

So he did understand.

Zia sidled up to Skye and put an arm around her shoulder. "Don't worry about this ado, Devi. I'll take good care of her. Make sure she stays out of trouble."

"Oh that makes me feel better."

Zia tapped her chin thoughtfully. "You know, Skye, maybe we should lobby for a change in the sky jumping regs—push for a 5K leap?"

Buyu groaned. "Zia, I always knew you were the smart one. But before you two plunge to your deaths, let's go collect that meal Chef Carlisle owes us. We've got reservations in fifteen minutes."

Skye laughed. She let go of Devi's hands, and shrugged out from under Zia's arm. "Ord! We're going."

Devi slipped off the railing. "Hey." He touched her shoulder. "You're sure it's okay?"

"Sooth." And it was.

Other Books by Linda Nagata

Skye Object 3270a is Linda Nagata's first work of young-adult fiction. All other books listed below are written for the general marketplace.

The Red Trilogy
    The Red: First Light
    The Trials
    Going Dark

The Nanotech Succession:
    Tech-Heaven (Prequel)
    The Bohr Maker
    Deception Well
    Vast

Stories of the Puzzle Lands
    The Dread Hammer
    Hepen the Watcher

Other Story Worlds:
    The Last Good Man
    Light And Shadow: eight short stories
    Limit of Vision
    Memory
    Goddesses & Other Stories
    The Wild

About the Author

Linda Nagata grew up in a rented beach house on the north shore of Oahu. She graduated from the University of Hawaii with a degree in zoology and worked for a time at Haleakala National Park on the island of Maui. She has been a writer, a mom, a programmer of database-driven websites, and a publisher and book designer. She lives with her husband in their long-time home on the island of Maui.

Find her online at MythicIsland.com.

Made in United States
Orlando, FL
14 May 2022